Fender
LIZARDS

Joe R. Lansdale

SUBTERRANEAN PRESS 2015

First Edition

ISBN
978-1-59606-717-2

Subterranean Press
PO Box 190106
Burton, MI 48519

subterraneanpress.com

For Karen. And in one way, aren't they all?

∭

Wish I had a river I could skate away on.

Joni Mitchell

You might not think some of this story is real because there are bits of it that are hard to believe, but you got my word it's the real thing from beginning to end. I want to get it all down now before time causes me to add stuff to juice it up, as if this story needs any juicing.

That lying part happens. I know. My father, he was a liar. He could tell a true thing until it became a lie. Just kept adding on and making it bigger, and bringing in things that didn't happen, pushing out things that did, so that eventually all you had left was the lie part, and he didn't know the difference anymore.

I hope that sort of thing isn't inherited.

I'm going to take the high road and say it isn't.

I'm going to say this is the true business, from beginning to end. I'm going to say my name is Dorothy Sherman and I'm telling it like it is. I'm going to say my friends call me Dot, and I prefer my enemies not to call me at all.

Is this a great adventure? Well, no one goes to the moon or climbs a high mountain. But for me it's an adventure. It's my day to day life.

My father once gave me some advice that I've mostly taken to heart. It hasn't got a whole lot to do with my story, not directly, but in it are words of wisdom, and I think it points out that my family is a family of philosophers.

He said, "Remember, in your diet, it takes a bit of grease to aid digestion." And the other bit of advice he gave was, "Save your money, cause I ain't gonna be giving you none extra."

That was the certain truth. He didn't even give us the basic, let alone extra. He took off when I was twelve and my brother was five. Did that thing you hear about. Went out for a pack of cigarettes and didn't come back.

For a long time I imagined he had gone to the store and they didn't have any, so he drove over to Longview to get some. After a week or two, I figured someone would have had some cigarettes, and he'd have had time to come back, even if he had to walk back with both feet in a bucket full of hardened cement.

I'm seventeen now, five years since I overheard Dad's words of wisdom, just shortly before his departure on a world wide cigarette run, and now he's been long gone and I got me a job as a roller skating waitress at a drive-in fast-food spot that's open twenty-four hours a day and is called the Dairy Bob. That's right, the Dairy Bob.

Guy runs it is named Bob. Nice enough guy, thirty or so. When he went into business he didn't know what to call his place. He said he grew up going to Dairy Queens, decided to call it Dairy something or another, but couldn't decide on a name. Finally, he decided on his own name. Bob.

The Dairy Bob is just off highway 59, and I bet that name throws a lot of folks driving through, looking over and seeing the sign, thinking: What the heck?

Bob is there at all hours, and he has an assistant manager named Marilyn who works just long enough for him to sleep, which seems to be very few hours a night. I don't see her much. So little I wouldn't recognize her on the street, I figure. I seem to be there mostly when Bob is.

It's not the worst job in the world, but it wears a body out by the end of the day. My ankles and calves hurt the most, but it

doesn't do my butt any good either, except in the looks department. When you skate six hours a night, it tends to tighten up
the old bean bags.

That's my shift, six hours a night. When I turn eighteen, I
can get eight hours, officially, though there is a bit of off the books
work now where I work more hours and get paid in cash. I try to
pretend right before I go to sleep at night that I'm going to get my
GED, which everyone calls the Good Enough Diploma, and then
some college. Some kind of real degree, instead of a nurse's helper,
or whatever they're called, or beautician, or a court reporter.

They're good enough ambitions, and it's all honest work, but
every girl I know who dropped out of school, or got knocked up
and usually had their fella run off, ended up doing one of those
three, and living in a trailer, which, in fact, I already do. I guess
it's actually a mobile home, but my mother calls it a trailer, and
so do we all. Anyway, I live in one. Me, my Mom, little brother
Frank, and Grandma. It sucks. I'm always wishing our home
was wider. When I meet Grandma coming down the hall on the
way to the bathroom—and I should note she's not the type that
misses any meals—we almost have to wrestle and do some kind
of acrobatics to get by one another.

I don't want to end up like my older sister, Raylynn, neither. She's twenty-three and has a different daddy than us. He got
killed when she was small and she doesn't remember him. He was
working under a car held up with an old-style jack, and a dog run
up against it. It popped loose and the car dropped on him and
crushed him. The dog was all right though. Mama said he died a
year later, peaceful like, out in the yard with one leg cocked up so
he could take in the spring time sun.

Raylynn's got her own trailer and she works at the Dairy
Bob with me. She tried to be a beautician, but the women she
worked on weren't happy. Two of them had their hair fall out

and something in one of the chemicals Raylynn mixed up caused another to get a kind of ear fungus that was resistant to medication. A lawsuit followed, and the beauty shop lost. It didn't exactly put her in high demand, and she was soon fired with what she calls Extreme Prejudice.

She went to work at the Dairy Bob then. She got me on. She hates it there. She says what future she might have had has come and gone and left no shadow.

She's smart enough, when she uses her head, but a lot of time her brain seems to be on vacation. She's pretty, but she ought to have been smarter and less pretty, cause she shacked up with this boy when she was sixteen, just ran off from home because she was, as my mother mocked, "In luuuuve."

Only thing was, the fella wasn't in love, least not when he heard there was a baby coming. That would be my nephew, Jake, who is a couple years old now. Anyway, the fella decamped and headed for parts unknown. All he left Raylynn was some old socks with holes in the toes and a bit of change down in the couch cushions, and that was purely by accident.

Pretty soon Raylynn was living back with us, least till she had Jake. After he was born, that family closeness didn't work out so good, so she got a job at the Dairy Bob, and then rented a trailer that was even smaller than the one we lived in.

She met a fella named Tim, and he proved consistent with her taste in men. Pretty soon after they started living together, she got her belly full of baby again, and Tim came down with back trouble, what he stupidly called, "the lumbargo."

Pretty soon he wasn't working. Raylynn was bringing in all the money. He sits home in his undershorts with a case of cheap beer and the Game Show Channel. He keeps a package of batteries near by in case the channel changer goes dead and he might have to get up. This way he's always well positioned.

Raylynn rags about him all the time to me, but she stays with him. And when her second baby, that would be my niece, Constance, came along, she didn't get any rest either. Things got worse. The babies stay at the day care center and that sucks up all the money she makes because Tim doesn't like to change diapers. It being women's work and all, and the fact you might have to put down a bottle of beer or the channel changer for about five minutes. He just sits at home, waiting on a managerial position, or maybe an opening for nuclear physicist.

I feel bad about it, but I keep hoping a truck will hit him, maybe drag him for a couple of miles. It's not a nice thing for a girl to think about, but, there you have it. At least in my mind I can be savage. I read a self-help book once that talked about pent-up anger, and I think I got plenty of that. Not to mention self-esteem issues, which I make up for by false bravado. False bravado was also in the book. It wasn't a very good book, but I remember it talking about that kind of stuff.

Because of that, who am I to bitch about other people's lives? Guess a seventeen-year-old high school dropout with plans to take the GED when she can study up for it, isn't exactly something an outsider might look at and visualize as someone with a big future.

I got to pay for most of the stuff I want, including food, cause Mama, she works at the Dollar Store, and it don't pay enough to do anything with, and Grandma has a bad leg that hasn't healed up right. It's no big deal. She has slight limp. When people ask her what happened, she tells them she got drunk and fell off the porch.

Well, we don't have a porch, and she doesn't drink either, but that's how Grandma is. She slipped coming out of the bathtub and her leg went this way, and the rest of her considerable self went the other. That didn't do her leg any good, of course. My brother, Frank, he's ten, and we've got hopes for him. He's kind of a nerd, but, hey, what the heck, as Mom says, "Whatever makes you happy and don't make a mess on the living room rug."

By the way, the job I got at the Dairy Bob, it's got a kind of title. Bob calls us girls Fender Lizards. It's an old term, from the fifties, or so he says, and has to do with roller skating waitresses skirting around car fenders all day, and sometimes running into them. I can show you the bruises.

I kind of like that name, Fender Lizard, and refer to myself that way any chance I get. It's a great conversation starter, and I've hit it up with a couple boys more than once by just using that title for myself.

I think they think it's something nasty.

Just for the record, I didn't go out with any of them.

Problem is, you're a drop out, boys you meet all seem to be drops outs too, and proud of it. Always got weed-eater haircuts, jailhouse tattoos, and junk jewelry in their faces, like they had some kind of accident while fly fishing.

I'm not hip. I don't like tattoos and I don't like all that crap in a boy's face. Or a girl's. I can go for ear rings now and then. I do have pierces there, on the ear lobes, but there's girls I know who have been pierced and have put hardware where stuff sure don't need to go.

My mama once gave me some advice on this matter, and like the advice from my daddy, I treasure it.

"Don't be poking holes in your basement, Dot."

Remember, I said my people are a bunch of philosophers.

Anyway, that's my family and that's my job and that's my life, such as it is.

I'm going to pause here a moment while envy sets in on you.

***N**ow, there was a* bright spot that come into all this, kind of like a strong light shining through a greasy sack, and it was in the form of my father's brother, Uncle Elbert, who I had never met, and for that matter, neither had none of the family. We didn't even know he had a brother, and I didn't know it was a bright spot at the time, but we'll come back to that.

He came to visit, bringing with him an old green Dodge Caravan that looked like it had been driven around the world, including under the ocean. He had it stuffed with all manner of junk, and he said to me later that he had been living out of it. This was easy to believe, because the side door of the van was slid back when I got out of my car, and I could smell an odor coming from it that was enough to make a skunk stagger and fall. It was late at night, me just off work, and I could hear him before I saw him good, because I had my window down on account of my air-conditioner doesn't work. He had a kind of sweet voice for a man. Not overly high or squeaky, but a little less of the bass and the brashness in it than the usual X-Y chromosome event. He was, as I heard Bob once refer to a man he knew, one of them that "had lied many a gal out of her charms and the contents of her wallet."

Anyway, there he was. This man I had never seen before, and neither had any of our family. He was sitting out in the yard with my Mama, Grandma, and my booger-picking brother, perched in lawn chairs so old that to sit in them was to take your life into your own hands.

He was an old man to me, but I suppose you could say he was a pretty good looker if you were about forty-five and hard up and maybe about six drinks past being in the bag. He had black hair, dyed I presumed—looked like shoe polish to me—and real sharp features and kind of full lips. He looked like a man that was happy all the time, which is something always makes me cautious. Daddy was like that, but if he had truly been happy he wouldn't have run off like a thief in the night.

I concluded all this in a flash, observing him in the bug light which hung on the outside of the trailer by the door. Uncle Elbert was drinking a beer and talking ninety miles an hour with a cigarette wiggling in one corner of his mouth. He didn't even take it out to talk or sip the beer.

I hate cigarettes, so I figured I'd hate him. Figured he'd be one of them that would give me a story about how he had the right to smoke because he was an American and such, like I had just dropped in from Armenia or some such place. I guess that's okay, long as its left outside of my house or where I'm eating. When I don't smoke, I don't offend anyone with my air, unless maybe I've been eating onions and I'm standing real close, but smokers offend anyone who doesn't smoke, or who has paid twelve bucks for a good meal and now has to eat and taste smoke so they can make sure some tobacco-lover has their rights, which, far as I'm concerned, end at the tip of my highly attractive young nose.

Anyway, I don't like cigarettes. Hadn't my old man gone out for cigarettes and not come back? Those darn things were a nuisance and cancer-causer and led to disappearance.

So, I'm out of the car and walking up, and here's this strange man. I heard Mama and Grandma laughing at something he said, and as I walked over, he stood up, said, "My goodness. This is the little daughter? Why, isn't she just the prettiest thing? She looks like you, Alma."

That's my mother's name, Alma.

And I did look like her. When she was young. I've seen pictures.

"Come on over here," Mama said, as if I might swerve off and head in the direction of the African continent at a dead run.

When I got up close, the man said, "I'm your uncle. Uncle Elbert, baby darling."

He kind of nabbed me then, put his arm around me. He smelled a little ripe.

"I been sitting here just waiting to meet you," he said. "I got to see your sister next."

He snuggled me up close, his arm heavy around me, said with breath like an ash tray, "It's just so damn good to be in the bosom of my family."

"Oh, Elbert," Mama said, "don't be cussing like that."

I almost laughed. All the cussing I ever learned I learned from her, usually all the words at once when she mashed her finger, stumped her toe, or her football team lost.

"Well, hell," Uncle Elbert said, "it is good. Ain't it?"

I didn't know what to say to that, so I smiled, trying to make it big and real, but I think it looked more like a possum barring its teeth.

"He gave me a pocket knife," my little brother said.

"That's nice," I said.

"It's got one blade missing," Frank said. "The big one. It's just got the little one."

"It's just a starter knife," Elbert said.

"Elbert," Mama said, like she had known him all her life. "You and Dot ought to run down to the Wal-Mart and get some sodas and things. I haven't got any real food for a guest. And it's the only thing around here open twenty-four hours."

I thought, that's nice. I don't even know this guy, and neither does she, or for that matter anyone else, and she wants me and him to head out to the store and buy some sodas.

"That sounds like a fine idea," he said. "We maybe can get some popcorn and the like. But Alma, I'm not a guest. I'm family."

"We won't need any popcorn tonight," Mama said. "We've had supper."

"I haven't," I said.

"Didn't you eat at the Dairy Bob?"

"Ha," Uncle Elbert said. "The Dairy Bob. That's funny."

To make a long story short, me and him went in my car to the store.

S*o, there I was*, driving along with someone who could have been a serial killer or an escaped lunatic or a used car salesman, sent on a mission by my mother to get us snacks.

As we drove, I asked what I figured Mama had already asked. "Where in the hell is my daddy?"

"Well, darling. I don't know. I haven't seen him in some time. I saw him some years back, shortly after he darted out on you folks. He told me all about you. He loves you."

"He sure knows how to show it."

"He chickened out," Elbert said.

"On what?"

"On life."

"How could he?"

"He was scared he wasn't doing right by you and the family."

"Now that's something," I said. "He left us to do better by us?"

"I'm not preaching his doctrine," Elbert said, "I'm just telling you what it is."

"Did he say what he had planned?" I asked.

"He didn't. And I haven't seen him since. He stayed with me at my place, and then the next morning he was gone, and so was my cookie jar."

"He stole your cookies?"

"The jar and the money in it," Elbert said. "I was out of cookies. I don't reckon thirty-five dollars got him all that far."

"So how come we're just now hearing from you?"

"Good question, darling. Good question. And I don't have a good answer."

"You were living where?"

"In San Antonio, Texas," he said.

"That close, and we haven't seen you until now?"

"It's five hours southwest of here," he said.

"Now you're starting to sound like Daddy. He never did like an inconvenience. Wow. Five hours. That's less than my shift at the Dairy Bob."

"Reckon I am sounding like him. All right. Here's the truth. Not long after your daddy showed up I decided that robbing the local bank wouldn't be all that big a sin, as they had foreclosed on a lot of good folks, one of them folks being me."

"You're a bank robber?"

"I tried. But I guess you need a gun for that. I didn't bring one. I just sounded threatening. I even used some harsh language. Not as effectively as I had presumed."

"What happened?"

"They wouldn't give me any money," Elbert said. "There was an argument. I asked for the money. I never said I had a weapon, but I acted like I had one. But the teller, a young lady with the bluest eyes you've ever seen... Well, not as blue as yours."

"My eyes don't matter," I said. "Just go on with the story."

"She wasn't intimidated," he said. "She wouldn't hand the money over. I had to leave. But they had already called the cops and they caught me down the street. I made the mistake of parking my car too far away because they didn't have a parking meter that worked. I parked at one first, but it wouldn't take coins. It was jammed up. So I parked down a ways where there wasn't one."

"You didn't want to break a parking meter law, but you tried to rob a bank and parked your getaway car too far away?"

"Kind of silly, huh?"

"I'll say."

"The law and the judge thought I ought to go to prison for awhile, so I did. I mean, they didn't give me a choice."

"I guess not," I said.

"I didn't have the parking meter fine to worry about though," he said.

"Good to know you got that going for you."

"So, that's where I been, and that's why I didn't come see you when you was little."

"You just got out of prison?" I asked.

"I did a little stretch up at Huntsville, got out, tried to get a job, but didn't do all that good at it. I opened up a little detective agency for awhile in San Antonio."

"Detective agency? You're a criminal."

"Wannabe criminal, to be precise. I didn't rob anybody. Remember, I didn't get any money."

I turned off the main highway into the Wal-Mart lot and found a parking place. I turned off the lights, but I didn't get out. "A wannabe criminal is the same thing as a successful criminal in my book. The same thing, Elbert. I hope calling you Elbert is okay, because I don't want to call you uncle. I don't want to call you at all, actually. Even on the phone."

"You speak your mind, don't you?"

"I do."

"Good. I like that."

"It don't matter if you do. It's not like it's on the auction block. You can take my attitude or not."

"That's quite a way for a young woman to talk to her elder."

"You're an elder I don't know all that well, and in fact, I don't know I should have rode over here with you to the store. Sometimes I think my mama leaves her brain in her dresser drawer."

"You don't think I'm some kind of pervert, do you?" he asked.

"I don't know what you are. Not yet. But I do know you're a bank robber."

"Attempted bank robber."

"I told you how I feel about that," I said. "Unsuccessful or not, you are still a bank robber. And you can understand right now you don't smoke in my car."

"I wasn't going to."

"Just in case the thought came up," I said.

"It won't come up," he said. "That was my last one back there at the trailer. Truth is I never smoked any before tonight. Well, some when I was young that I got caught for and got in trouble at school. I was nervous tonight, so I bought a pack. It just stinks up your clothes. I can smell it on me."

"So can I," I said. "But I still don't know why you're here."

Elbert nodded. "One day I got to thinking that I had family I didn't even know. Did you know you had an uncle?"

"It wasn't mentioned," I said. "Dad wasn't a big talker about anything that mattered, just stuff that didn't. If mama knew about you, she never mentioned it."

"Your mama was very nice to me," Elbert said. "And she didn't know about me. I can't believe Jethro would never mention me or run off like he did."

"Well, he did," I said.

"Thing is, darling. I want to try and make up some of what your father didn't do. And I want to make something of my life, and I thought being a real uncle to you might be part of it."

"You didn't have a job when you came here, did you?" I said. "I mean, this isn't a vacation, is it?"

"No."

"And you don't have a place to live?" I said.

"No. I didn't."

"So, what you really did is come here to get some free meals and a spot to hole up."

"It's more than that."

"Yeah, but it's some of that, isn't it?"

"You are very tough, darling."

"I'm very tired," I said. "I'm very worn out. And I don't know you any better than a cat in the shadows."

Elbert was unfazed.

"Shall we go in the store?" he said.

I opened the door and got out and started toward the store without waiting for him to follow.

Such was the beginning of our friendship.

"So you skate the food out?" Uncle Elbert said. "On a tray?"

"That's right," I said. We were back at the trailer, sitting at the table. Mama had fixed him a spot on the couch and moved Frank, whose bedroom was usually the couch, to a pallet on the floor in her bedroom.

"Well, I'll be," Elbert said, looking legitimately surprised. "When I was a kid, they had them kind of things, but I didn't know they still did it. And the place is called the Dairy Bob?"

"Yeah. Still called that."

"I used to skate."

"That's nice," I said.

Our little talk hadn't discouraged his friendliness in the least, and after he had a microwaved Hungry Man Dinner in him, his second meal of the night, he felt pretty fit again.

It was real late and we were in the living room and Mama and Grandma and Frank had wandered off to bed, and made Frank go, and I was still trapped, listening to Uncle Elbert. The conversation had dwindled to the dregs, but I had to admit, he was a likeable enough guy, if you could put the bank robbing aside, and the fact that he was a blowhard.

"Well, I got to get to bed now," I said.

"Sure," he said. "Do you make good money?"

"So-so."

"Well, so-so is better than none."

"I suppose," I said. "You're not looking for a loan, are you?"

"I could use a couple bucks," he said.

I glared at him.

"I'm just kidding," he said. "You going to take the GED?"

"Mama told you about that?"

"She did. You going to take it?"

Uncle Elbert had a way of tagging a conversation at the end of each sentence so you were always nailed for further comment.

"Mama really does talk a lot," I said.

"I have a year of college."

"Good for you," I said. "It certainly has proved fruitful, hasn't it? Goodnight." I started for the bedroom.

"It is a good night, I'll say that. I really am glad to be home."

I thought: You mean you're glad to be in our home. But I didn't say that. I said, "Yeah. Well, you got blankets and pillows. The couch is pretty comfortable. Goodnight. And leave something in the refrigerator for the rest of us."

"That's just mean," he said.

I darted for the end room, which is the one I share with Grandma, and eased inside and closed the door before he could tag another line. Safe at last.

I actually figured that come morning I'd go in there to find him gone and all the food eaten up and maybe something stolen. It was a cheap price to pay to get rid of him, I thought.

It was dark in the bedroom, but I knew my way around, and I tried to be quiet about it, because Grandma is a light sleeper.

When I got into bed, which is a little rack in the corner of the room, I heard Grandma shift in her bed like a hippopotamus trying to make a wallow.

"What you think of him?" she asked.

"Kind of odd him just showing up all of a sudden out of the thin air." I started to add: "And did you know he's a bank robber?" But it was too late to get all that started.

"He's got your father's nose," Grandma said.

"Won't he need it?" I said.

"What?"

"His nose. If he's got my father's nose, won't my father need it?"

"What?"

"Never mind."

I crawled under the blankets and pulled them up tight to my neck and tried to come up with something good to think about, some kind of thing that would spur a good dream. I almost had hold of something when I heard Grandma laugh.

"Oh, I get it," she said.

"What?"

"About the nose," she said. "I get it now. It was a joke."

"Good for you, Grandma," I said.

She snickered a little and I closed my eyes again.

I was sleeping till about nine or ten in the mornings. I'd get up, have breakfast or an early lunch, and then go into town to run errands even if I didn't have any. After that I went to work. The shifts change. But right then I was on the six to midnight.

Breakfast or lunch isn't much of nothing, and is often the same thing. Toast or some kind of cereal, usually with enough sugar in it to make a diabetic let out with a scream and drop dead after about two spoonfuls.

For supper I can get something free at the Dairy Bob. Bob lets us workers have one meal on the house, and gives us discounts on others. I find you can also slip a French fry or something or another now and then without it really hurting anybody, especially if you don't get caught. You get caught, you get yelled at, and Bob threatens to take it out of your pay.

How much would that be? A penny a French fry? Five cents an onion ring?

Anyway, so far it's just been threats and he hasn't done nothing about it.

But Bob, he's all right. When I got my driver's license and was able to quit riding to work with my sister, Bob gave me five dollars for gas, and a hot dog with French fries for what he called a "car driving present."

Personally, I think they ought to make this a holiday. Everybody gets their license, they should get five dollars and something to eat that isn't good for you. Wouldn't that be cool? All of this at a restaurant of your choice.

Anyway, this was my life, day in and day out, and then one morning Raylynn didn't come to work, and things changed. She didn't call in or nothing, just didn't show up.

Bob phoned over to her trailer from the Dairy Bob a couple of times, but didn't get an answer. I called twice and didn't get nothing either. He told me she ought to have called in, then told me I had to take her shift, which was kind of silly, since we worked the same time slot. I guess he meant I had to do her work and mine too.

During my break, I called on my cell phone, which I figured I'd lose shortly because I hadn't paid my bill, but I didn't get her to answer either.

It bothered me. Not big time, but some. It wasn't like Raylynn to miss work, and if she was going be late, she was good about calling in, and she always had a good lie if she was going take a day off. She didn't just go in for I'm sick, she had really good stories that managed to fall slightly short of I've got rabies from a rabid cat bite, or I been kidnapped by aliens and have had an anal probe. Or I'll have to miss next week too because I have to go back with the aliens for a follow up.

During the day she'd leave the kids at the day care because she couldn't leave them with Grandma who had a habit of falling asleep at odd moments. Mama had to work, and had warned her she'd already raised her kids and wasn't looking for a second shift.

I called over to the day care and found out she hadn't brought the kids in.

With Raylynn not calling, and not coming in late, and not being at home when we called, and the kids not being at day care, well, that pissed Bob, because he was thinking she took a holiday.

Me, I was worried. I wanted to drive over there, but we were covered up in customers, and Bob didn't want me to go.

One car full of people had me going back for this and that, and ordering more, and getting new drinks and such. They run up a good bill. When they paid, they told me, like they were big spenders, "Keep the change," which turned out to be twenty-two cents and some pocket lint.

I skated back inside and checked my cell. Raylynn hadn't called. I told Sue when she skated up that I was worried. Sue is the sweetest girl you could meet. She's all Southern in attitude, but she's part Pakistani and Mexican, and she said there's a few Irish folk in her background somewhere; my guess is a Leprechaun. She has smooth, dark skin that doesn't know a pimple, the greenest eyes you've ever seen and flame-red hair. I've never seen anyone that looked like her unless it was out of a comic book and they got their looks from radioactivity or something.

Well, I told her I was worried about Raylynn, and she gave me that sort of sleepy-eyed look of hers, said I ought to go no matter what Bob thought. "It ain't like this job is so coveted that you ain't back in thirty minutes you're gonna have to fight off the Employment office trying to stick in someone new."

There was a truth to that. Hard as it was to come by a job, there weren't many who wanted to be skating fast-food waitresses, considering how hard the work was and how little pay we got. It was a job only slightly coveted above field work.

Gay heard us talking, and she felt different about me running off to see how Raylynn was. She's this drop dead gorgeous black girl. She looks so good that when boys drive into the Dairy Bob and see her, it's like they've stumbled over a trip wire and a bomb has gone off. They practically shoot drool onto the windshield. She gets big tips and the like, and she's the worst worker ever because she's always on her cell phone. Bob doesn't fire her because there's a ton of boys and men that come there just to see her, like maybe they're coming to take a peek at the Mona Lisa, provided the Mona Lisa's black and built like an athlete and has more sex appeal than a football cheer squad and a couple of underwear models.

Gay already has interest from modeling agencies. She is very girly. Not stupid, but someone who puts what brains she has on the back burner. I think it's her style. I think she likes to make the guys think they're smart because she figures that's how a gal ought to be. I figure any guy wants a gal like that, he can just get an internet avatar.

She's certain the reason she washed out of college is she was so pretty no one took her seriously. Me and Sue and Raylynn think it had to do with her math scores and the fact she only went about once a week, and probably spent most of her time in a university bathroom talking on the phone.

Anyway, she didn't think I should go, but she didn't have any reason behind it. It wasn't like she was sharing her strong work ethic with me. My guess is she didn't want me to leave because she and Sue would have to take up my slack.

About eight o'clock, I told Bob I had had all I could take, and that I needed to drive over and see how Raylynn was, even if it chapped the Pope's rear end. I told him that with Sue and Gay he had enough help to do what was needed for a short time, as the crowd had slowed. I also added that I thought I could defy him because I was now independently wealthy with my twenty-two cent tip. I had hoped he would find that humorous, but he didn't.

He grumbled about it, but didn't give me a lot of flak, maybe because he thought I might take off anyway and not come back if he made me mad. Then he'd have to hire another girl that could skate, or if she couldn't, get one of the other girls to teach her. That would take time, and sometimes, you just couldn't teach a girl to skate, least not while carrying a tray loaded with chili dogs, drinks and onion rings. And there was that thing I mentioned before. It wasn't a job that everyone was salivating over. It looked fun, but it wasn't.

I told him I'd just run over and make sure everything was all right, then I'd come right back. I told him I thought she might have the ringer on her phone turned off, and that's why she wasn't picking up.

This didn't explain why she hadn't called, or about the kids, but it was all I could come up with.

My car is one of those that burns about a quart of oil a day. An old Ford. And I have to carry some cheap cans of oil in the trunk to run it so that it doesn't blow up. It probably wouldn't hurt if I had some spare parts in the trunk, along with a mechanic, but I got what I got.

I went out back of the Dairy Bob and put the hood up and poured a can of oil in, then drove over to see how Raylynn was doing. I was feeling nervous and itchy and gradually starting to feel afraid.

Being how it was dead solid summer in East Texas, it was still bright enough out to see good, though the sky was starting to show some dark. It was sticky hot too. Without an air conditioner in my car, I felt like I had been dried out in one of those big industrial dryers at the Washateria.

When I got over to the trailer park, I saw Raylynn's ride sitting out front, looking cleaner and shinier than it really was. It was just the way the light was on it. All the tires were flat.

I parked behind it, got out and looked at her tires. I figured they'd been knife poked. I could see the slits in the sides of the left rear and the left front. I decided I didn't need to examine the other side. I knew it was Tim's work without any real evidence.

I called out to her. That's a thing we do, us Shermans. It's an old country holdover. You get out of your car, and you start calling out the name of the person who lives there.

I've noted not everyone does that, and I asked Mama about it, and she said to ask Grandma, and I did, and she said, it's a holdover from the old days when a person rode up on a horse in the middle of the night, and you didn't know if it was friend or foe, so you wanted them to announce themselves right off. The other side of the coin was the person doing the announcing didn't want to startle nobody and get shot before they could knock on the door.

I didn't get an answer to my call, so I decided to be brave, but loud. I went up and knocked on the door and called out

Raylynn's name. Nobody answered. I knocked louder, and she still didn't answer. Neither did her boyfriend. If he was the one going to answer, I hoped he had on some pants, something other than his undershorts. But since his pickup wasn't there, I didn't figure he was home.

I walked around back and tapped on the window glass where the bedroom was. There was an air conditioner in the window next to the one I was tapping on. It was humming loudly. That could be why I hadn't been heard when I was calling and knocking at the front door. I tapped harder.

After a moment I heard stirring inside, and then the window came up. I could see Raylynn's shape in the dark room, and I could hear the baby crying.

"You done woke her up with all that knocking," she said.

"I was worried about you."

"I'm all right."

"You don't sound all right."

"I got a cold."

"A cold?"

"Yeah," Raylynn said. "A cold. You've heard of them."

"You sure are cranky," I said.

"I got to tend to the baby now," she said.

"Let me come in and help you."

"That's all right. You go on home."

"I've been at work," I said. "Like you're supposed to be."

"I didn't feel like coming today."

"So you didn't call, didn't answer your phone?"

"That's the size of it," she said. "Go back to work."

Raylynn reached to pull the window down, and as she did, she come into the light and I saw her face. She had dark spots on her cheeks and under her eyes. She looked like a raccoon that had survived being hit by a car.

"Heavens, Raylynn. What happened?"

She leaned back out of view, into the shadows of the darkened room. The baby cried louder.

"I had a fall in the night," she said.

"Looks to me like you fell half a dozen times," I said.

"Mind your own business," she said.

"Let me in or I'll knock the window glass out and crawl inside," I said.

I meant it, and she knew it. She may be the older sister, but I'm the tougher one.

"Come around front," she said, "and I'll let you in."

I went around. The door was open by the time I got there. Raylynn had the baby against her shoulder. She still hadn't turned on any lights.

I went inside and turned the kitchen light on and looked at her.

She was a little stooped and was marked up worse than she had appeared at first.

I said, "He hit you, didn't he?"

"This isn't a fashion statement," she said.

"Tell me," I said. "I want to hear you say it. He hit you."

"He did, and several times."

"You don't have to put up with that," I said.

"He gets mad now and then, but he gets over it."

"Yeah, but you got to get over getting hit," I said. "He's just got to get over being drunk. You don't have to put up with crap. This is ridiculous. You got to get out of here."

I went over to the refrigerator, got an ice tray out, plucked a towel down from the rack over the kitchen sink, and broke the tray open into it. I folded the towel around the ice, made Raylynn sit down. I gave her the cold damp towel and had her press it against her face.

"He can't find a job, and it frustrates him," Raylynn said.

"There's lots of folks can't find a job and are frustrated," I said, "but they don't have to hit people over it. Hitting you won't get him a job. Fact is, I think he could get one if he wanted it."

"He just doesn't want to do something humiliating."

"Yeah," I said. "He's quite the upper crust, isn't he?"

"I love him," Raylynn said.

"Please," I said.

"Well, you ain't in love," she said.

"No. And if what you got is love, then I don't want any."

Raylynn started to cry.

"Sorry, Raylynn," I said.

"It's all right," she said between sniffs. "I just don't know what to do."

Raylynn went in to check on Jake and to put the baby back in the crib. I went with her. We talked softly.

"I put them to bed early, and they went right to sleep," she said. "I think all the yelling and Tim hitting on me scared them."

"You think?"

"Don't make me feel worse than I do," she said.

"Sorry," I said.

Jake was asleep in the bed where Raylynn had been, and Constance was in her crib and had gone back to sleep even while she had been on Raylynn's shoulder. Constance was pretty big for the crib, but that's what they had.

We both stood and looked down at the baby. All I could think was that goon had hit my sister and the kids had been here to see it.

"He coming home tonight?" I said.

"I don't know," she said. "It's better he don't come back too soon, cause it just leads to more hitting if he hasn't got sober. If he has a day to think about things, he comes back and he's real sorry."

"He is, huh?"

"Yeah, and he means it."

"Every time?"

"You just don't understand," Raylynn said.

"No," I said. "I don't."

Raylynn and I talked briefly, but she hurt a lot and had to lay down. It wasn't anytime at all until she was asleep.

I went out in the yard. It was good and dark now. The air was cool. I leaned on my car and thought about things for a long time and looked at the sky. Finally I got in my car and drove down the street a piece and parked in a church parking lot, and walked back.

There were some rotting boards shoved up under the trailer from when Tim was going to build a porch off the front door instead of just having concrete steps. He had plans to screen it in so he could sit out there and smoke cigarettes and think about the jobs he didn't have, or being a rock star, or what have you, but of course he hadn't done a thing. The weather and bugs had been at the boards, and they had warped.

I pulled a short two-by-four out from under the trailer, a stout one that wasn't too warped. There was a lawn chair at the edge of the yard, under the shadow of a big oak. I pulled the chair up by the tree trunk and sat down and held the board.

It got late and I nodded off a little, but the sound of Tim's truck pulling into the drive woke me up. I watched from where I sat as he got out of his truck, weaving a bit, having been driving drunk as a pig in corn mash. He was feeling around in his pocket for his keys. He found them, waddled toward the steps. I got up with the two-by-four and walked up quick behind him.

"Timmy," I said. "Look at me."

He turned, and I swung that board really hard, clipped him across the knees. He made a noise and I hit him again. For legal purposes, I'll have to say I don't remember exactly how many times I hit him, but adding a personal note, it could be said maybe more times than I should have, but not anymore times than he needed.

When he was lying on the ground groaning, I squatted down close to his ear, and said, "You hit my sister again, or you ever touch the babies with the faintest bit of mean spirit in you, they're going to have to get a tow truck to get this board out of the spot where I'm gonna put it. You got me, Timmy?"

"You didn't have no call to do that," he said. And he tried to put his arms under him and get up.

I hit him again.

He lay down and was still. I was afraid for a moment I had killed him. I was kind of hopeful of it at the same time. "You still with me, Timmy?" I said.

He grunted.

I repeated my previous message.

"I'll get you too," he said.

"No," I said. "No, you won't."

I hit him again, and it was a pretty good lick, in the head. I know how that sounds, but all I can tell you is I didn't lean into it.

He didn't say anything, and I checked his pulse. He was still alive, just knocked out. I got the keys he dropped and put them in my pocket, went inside the trailer and woke Raylynn up.

"Timmy fell down," I said. "A couple of times."

"Fell down?" Raylynn said.

"A small two-by-four helped him," I said.

"Oh, Sis."

"Don't Oh, Sis me. Get the babies. We're leaving. Tim's face down in the yard. When he wakes up, I'm pretty sure he's going to be mad."

Raylynn surprised me by listening. She got up and got some things together, mostly stuff for the kids, and we went outside.

Tim was still on the ground. I took his keys out of my pocket and tossed them in the direction of the oak tree. Then with Raylynn carrying the baby, and me carrying her goods in a cardboard box, we walked down to my car in the church lot, and I drove us away from there.

On Tuesday I'm pretty ashamed about what I did to Tim, but the rest of the week I feel pretty good about it. At least that's how I felt the first week, and then Mama got a call from a lawyer and the word was passed to me. I was wanted in court. Tim had called the law on me. Mama said if I had to spend time in jail she'd be sure and bring me something to eat at least once a week, though it might be from the Dairy Bob. I think that was a sad kind of joke, but I wasn't sure. Grandma said I might find my father there, as she figured that's how he ended up. In prison.

I had two days before I had to show, cause the judge was on vacation.

On top of all that, Raylynn and her kids ended up in my bed, and I had to share with Grandma, which I did one night only. Grandma had a gas problem. Next night I made myself a pallet on the floor and slept there, managing to get a crick in my neck about every other day.

I didn't tell Elbert any of this, but with Raylynn and her kids moving in, and Mama being a blabbermouth, he knew all there was to know about it right away.

One morning I was having some toast, some milk and sugar mixed in with a drop of coffee. Elbert was sitting across the table from me, looking at me like an old dog that wanted to know if I was going to take him out to pee. He said, "So, you got to go to court?"

"Did Mama tell you my shoe size too?"

"Six."

"Seven," I said.

He smiled. "No. She didn't tell me. You did."

"Very funny," I said.

"Was it worth it?"

"Smacking Tim with a board?"

"Yep."

"You know," I said. "I think it was. It sure felt good hitting him, knowing what he had done to Raylynn. Yeah. I guess it felt all right. But, I'd still rather not go to jail."

"You won't go to jail," Elbert said. "You could, but I doubt you will, being young and all. The situation like it is. You might have to pay some kind of fine. Do some community work or something."

"I hope that's all," I said.

I sipped some coffee and got up and grabbed my skates and was starting out the door. Elbert, as he always did, tagged me with a conversation piece.

"You know," he said. "I used to skate."

"Did you also water ski? Or maybe leap barrels on a horse?"

"You have a bad attitude, Dot."

"I do. There it is. I have a bad attitude. Besides, you told me before you skated, so now you've told me twice."

I reached for the door knob.

"You can't go around hitting people with boards," he said.

"I don't go around hitting people with boards. Just him."

"Listen, I know you don't know me and probably don't think I know my ass from my elbow, but you're an angry girl. You keep on being angry, you'll be just like the guy you beat with a board. What's his name? Tim?"

"Yeah."

"You'll be like him."

"I'll turn into a guy that beats his girlfriend and sits around in his underwear drinking beer, watching game shows?"

Elbert sighed.

"Just listen to me briefly, and I'll let you go, and I'll have had my say on the matter. You should have just grabbed your sister and left. You waited on Tim, snuck up on him and clobbered him."

"I figured it would work out better that way. Really. I got to go."

"You have a chance to get out of here, out of this life, out of your background, like a bird flying out of a cage. But you're not careful, you'll be just what you don't like. I don't blame you for being angry. You're working hard. No high school education. Tough situation all around. But you got to quit blaming things and start fixing things."

"Is this ex-con advice on how to live my life?"

"Jail didn't make me better, but getting older did, and I can tell you, way you're acting, you're going to ruin any chance you got."

"I don't plan to rob a bank," I said.

"Look. I don't blame you. I'm not saying I know much, and I'm not saying Tim didn't have it coming. I might have done the same thing. I'm just saying you got a lot more going on than you think. You got a brain. You got a heart, if an angry one. You got potential. I just want you to have your shot."

"That's nice," I said. "I'm going to work. I got the morning shift for a while. Day's the day I switch over."

I went outside and stood by the long concrete drive. I put on my skates and started skating. I liked to do that when I could, even if I was about to go to work and skate all day. I love the skates. I love being on them. I felt in those moments as if I was part girl and part machine. It was a clean feeling of being one with the wind. When I skated free like that, not carrying trays, or thinking about orders or tips, I felt swift and powerful. It's a wonderful feeling, skating along with the wind in your face and the wheels on the skates whirling.

I only skated awhile, but it helped me feel better.

When I came back up the drive, I stopped at my car and opened the door and took off my skates and put on my shoes, and with them I put back on my worries.

I tossed my skates on the passenger seat beside me, climbed in behind the steering wheel, looked down at my blue jean covered knees and just sat there, even though I knew my work time was starting to tick. Bob was already mad at me for leaving work the other day, though truth was he wasn't all that mad. Unlike Elbert, he thought what I had done was pretty neat and gave me a few pointers on how to crack a man's ankles when he's down so he can't get up and chase you.

I filed those pointers away.

I thought about what Elbert said too. About what I could do, what I could accomplish. And that I was smart and had an angry heart.

I figured it was easy for someone to talk about things I could do, but a lot harder for me to actually do them. Sometimes I felt like I was a rat in one of those cages with a wheel in it and I was inside the wheel. Running, faster and faster, but just like that rat, I wasn't really getting anywhere.

And the rat didn't have an appointment with a judge.

"**D**o you think they'll send you to the Big House," Sue said that morning while we were at work. She was joking, but it didn't strike me as all that funny.

We were both outside of the Dairy Bob. I was on the morning shift, but today I was putting in extra time to make back money I had lost from when I bailed on Bob. It was just an hour or so extra a day for a week, but I had to come in even more early than usual when I was on the morning shift. The breakfast crowd with their sausage and biscuits and coffee were a real pain in the neck. Worse than the lunch rush. I really wasn't supposed to work that much according to law, but I wouldn't tell if Bob didn't. He paid me in cash when I did extra hours, off the books. I needed it. The last check, due to my missing hours, had been a little slim. After I gave mama some of it, there wasn't enough change left to rattle in my pocket.

Me and Sue had been skating food out all morning. Gay was primping in the bathroom. There were other girls and other shifts, but we didn't work with them normally, unless someone swapped out a shift or some such thing. Or, like I said, I got some sneaky hours off the books.

Today we were working with some of the other girls. We didn't know them well. That made things difficult. Me and Sue and Gay and Raylynn worked well together, even if Gay was kind of an airhead sometimes and took the wrong car, stepped on our toes that way.

Raylynn was inside working the tables. She was still getting over some body blows Tim had laid on her, and it was easier to work the tables than to skate. Skating, unlike what you might think, takes it out of you.

Raylynn said that when Tim was hitting her to the body, he'd say, "That there's an upper cut. That there's a hook."

He was some piece of work, that Tim.

"They send me to the pen," I said, "put a file in a cake and bring it to me."

"You bet," Sue said, nodding that head of thick, red hair. "Except I can't bake."

We were leaning against the wall on the far side of the Dairy Bob, waiting on customers to show up, catching a few moments of rest, trying not to let our skates slip out from under us.

"I want to do to my daddy what you did to Tim," Sue said.

I knew Sue's home life wasn't all that good, but I tried not to pry. I knew her father hit her mother. And he drank. He'd been to anger counseling, but he got in a fight with the anger management guy, so that hadn't worked out. The anger management guy was now in anger management.

"I was thinking when he goes to bed one night, I'm just going to get a board and go to work on him," Sue said. "Just like you."

I sighed and looked out at the highway. A bright red, low-slung car I'd never be able to afford drove by. I knew it wouldn't be stopping anywhere like the Dairy Bob, or anyplace in town. It was driving on through to some place better.

I looked at Sue. "You don't want to do that."

"He has it coming," Sue said. "Just like Tim did."

"No doubt. But you don't want to do it."

Holy cow, I thought. I'm sounding just like Elbert.

"You did it," she said.

"And I'm seeing a judge, and I may be sharing a cell with someone that makes me wash out their little white things."

"You ain't going to prison, and you know it," she said. "I was just kidding. This is East Texas. They might give you a medal."

"Had Tim been threatening Raylynn," I said. "Had he come there angry, then I'd have been okay doing it. I could sleep fine at nights. But I snuck up on him."

"So?"

"Well, it's not the sneaking that bothers me. It's that me and Raylynn could have left out of there long before Tim come home. I laid in wait, as they say."

"I can live with laying in wait," Sue said. "I can live with Daddy being asleep and me sneaking up on him."

"You think it'll make you feel better," I said. "And it will. Right at first. But later it won't. You won't like that you were able to do it. You ought to get your Mama and get out of there."

"She won't go," Sue said. "I ask her to leave. But she won't."

"I know," I said, using my Mama's mocking voice: "She's in luuuuuve."

"Yeah," Sue said. "That's it. And I feel so damn trapped, Dot. I want out and I don't know how to get out. If I got out, I wouldn't know what to do with myself. It's like when there's a parakeet in a cage and the door's left open and it flies out the window and the other birds peck it to death because it smells like humans, or it starves to death because it's used to bird seed in a tray. I feel like one of those birds. I get out, I won't know where to go."

"You'll know this much," I said, finding myself rephrasing Elbert's lines. "You won't be in a cage."

"So, you're saying it's all right to starve or get pecked to death?"

"I don't know what I'm saying," I said. "I'm not the right person to ask for advice. And while we're at it, I'm really no expert on parakeets and their life outside the cage."

ater that day, during the lunch run, a bunch of boys showed up in a nice car. All of them were good looking and well dressed, early college age. Sophomores were my guess. They looked like their biggest worries were which of their shoes they should throw away.

I skated out to the car, but Gay got things crooked, which is often the case, and muscled in. It was my turn and my possibility at a tip, but she was there first.

It irritated me, but I didn't mention it. I'd grab the next one. I didn't want to say anything to her, because now everyone was pretty sure I'd take a board to them, and it wasn't any fun working with people who thought you might at heart be a mass murderer.

I skated back inside the Dairy Bob. There was nothing shaking there that wasn't being covered by Raylynn and Sue at that moment, so I stood on my skates by the counter, using one hand to hold onto it and steady myself.

Bob was behind the counter taking money, working the register for a couple of guys. When he was finished with them and they went out, Bob came over and put his elbows on his side of the counter, said, "What kind of board did you use?"

"What?" I said.

"What kind of board did you use? On that kid you hit."

"For heaven's sake," I said.

"Really. What kind?"

"A two-by-four."

"Oak?"

"Do I look like someone who knows lumber?"

"Seasoned good?" he asked.

"Yeah. It was seasoned."

"A good seasoned piece of wood can take a lot of abuse," Bob said.

"I don't think I was worried about the wood all that much," I said. "Now that I think about it, it might have been a little wormy."

The door opened and the driver from the car full of boys Gay had stolen from me came in. He found a table and sat down. I glanced out at his car. The other boys were still in it and Gay was leaning in the window on the now empty driver's side, flashing her great smile, her butt cocked up in the air. It was a pose. Something she was good at. Already she had modeling assignments for J.C. Penny's and such, so she knew what looked good and what didn't. She was supposed to sign up with a modeling agency out of Austin in a few months. At least that was the rumor. Me, I'd still be lugging burgers on a tray.

She aggravated me, but I didn't know if it was because she was so beautiful and confident about it, or because I thought she was a little light in the brains and a bitch. I was on the fence.

I skated over to the table where the guy from the car had sat down. I pulled my pad and pen from my apron pocket, said, "What would you like?"

He looked at me. Oh, he was fine. Green eyes and black hair, dark skin, so smooth it looked as if it didn't have pores. He had broad shoulders and very nice teeth; the kind that cost money and made regular trips to the dentist. He made me realize I just had on some old ratty jeans, and not cool ratty, but just plain ratty, and a loose black tee-shirt.

He said, "Oh, I don't know. A hamburger, I guess."

"Cheese?"

"Sure," he said.

"You can put jalapeños on it," I said, "or mushrooms, but I don't recommend the mushrooms. They're dry and in a can. Cook just warms them in the microwave. They taste like scabs."

He smiled at me. "You eat a lot of scabs?"

"Told on myself," I said. "My favorite meal."

Yeah. I know. Not that good. But I was a little dazzled by his smile.

"After that description, I'm not sure I want a hamburger," he said.

"Sorry."

"Just kidding," he said. "Give me the cheeseburger, and put the jalapeños on it. I want mustard and mayonnaise. French fries with ketchup. And I'd like a bit of mayonnaise for the fries too. I like to dip the fries in both."

"I never heard of that," I said.

"My parents were Yankees. What you gonna do?"

I laughed. "You want it all, don't you?"

"I do," he said. "I like to taste a little of everything, if I can."

I was about to skate off with his order, but hesitated. I said, "All your friends are in the car. How come you came inside?"

"Because I've been here twice before and you never wait on me. I wanted you to wait on me."

"Me?"

"Yes," he said.

"Why?"

"Frankly, I think you're very attractive and I wanted to meet you."

"So, is this part of a college fraternity thing?"

"What?" he said.

"You know, some sort of thing where you have a chore to do, like come in and try and get a date with me to prove you can, but you really don't want one."

He stared at me. "If I asked you for a date I'd really want to go on a date."

"So, are you asking?" I said.

"Friday night. Seven o'clock. I can pick you up wherever you like."

I had to take a long moment to process that.

"That's good," I said. "Friday night's good. No... No it isn't. I work Friday night. Saturday I work too. I only have Sunday off."

Actually, I had plenty of time after my shift, but I knew Bob could change it on a whim, move me to nights, and I didn't want to ask him for anymore time off after bailing on him like I did.

"Then let's make it Sunday," he said.

"I don't even know your name."

"Herb Wagoner. Now you know it."

"Glad to meet you Herb. I'm Dot Sherman. But, I just realized I accepted a date from someone I don't know much about."

"Talking is how you find out. I'll take you someplace nice for dinner. We can talk over good food."

"Once again, I don't even know you," I said.

"But you accepted right away."

"I did, didn't I?"

"You did."

"Dang it," I said, and smiled. "Then I guess to keep my word I have to go."

"That's the way I see it," Herb said.

I was on cloud nine the rest of the day.

I kind of drifted through my work. I made several flubs, like skating the wrong tray out to the wrong car a couple of times. Bob started calling me Gay, which kind of hurt my professional pride as a Fender Lizard. This should of course been insulting to Gay, if she heard about it, but she didn't care if you complained about her. Unlike us, she knew she was merely passing through, this job a bit of a diversion before she left us and this town and its life behind.

When I came inside after finishing an order and was turning over the cash to Bob, he said, "What's wrong with you?"

"Nothing," I said.

"You don't seem yourself."

"Maybe it's because I'm going to court."

"You need a character witness, girl. You just ask me, I'll be there."

"That's nice of you, Bob."

"Oh, I'm not all that much in defense of your character. I just liked that you took care of Raylynn, who's the real worker. So, I owe you one."

He didn't smile when he said that, but I knew he was kidding. Mostly. Raylynn was a good worker.

"Nice," I said.

"Here," he said, pulling out four cardboard posters from behind the counter. "Tape these up."

I looked at the one on top. It had a painting of two women skating on it. They were shoving each other as they skated, looking beautifully furious. They wore white shorts and purple tops and had on high-laced white skates. Above the painting in broad letters were the words DARBY'S ROLLER CIRCUS with the CARNY KILLERS. Rides. Clowns. Exhibits. Fun for the whole family. Coming August seventh, MARVEL CREEK FAIR GROUNDS. Below all this was written in smaller letters: Darby's Roller Queens challenge all comers. Ten thousand dollar prize.

"What is this?" I asked.

"What it says," Bob said.

"Yeah, but I don't know what it means."

"It's a traveling roller derby and small carnival. They challenge local teams. If the local teams don't have anybody, they have another group of skaters with them. A kind of built-in team to play them. Its good entertainment. The women wear shorts."

"So people go to see this stuff?"

"Some do. The women wear shorts."

"You said that," I said.

"You don't get too old to like women in shorts."

"That's good to hear, Bob. You been to a roller derby?"

He shook his head. "Used to watch them on TV. They're not popular anymore, but they were for awhile."

"They actually give out a prize like this?" I asked. "Ten thousand dollars."

"What the sign says. But let me tell you something, kid. It's no easy take. They wouldn't offer a prize like that if they didn't figure they could beat whoever. Bunch of yokels on skates would have a hard time beating a trained team. And my guess is they're not only trained, but they're mean."

I looked at the poster and studied the women in the picture. They looked strong and confident, like maybe life didn't push them around without them pushing back. Sometimes I felt that way, but most of the time I thought I was kidding myself. I kind of envisioned myself at eighty-five bringing out food on trays, riding a wheelchair instead of skates.

I put up a couple of posters, taped them to the inside of the glass with the picture looking out at the drive through on one side, and a parking spot at the front. I put the third one on the glass door.

I skated outside and put the last poster in my car.

After that we were slammed for awhile. When that was over, all of us went out back and leaned on the wall, and Raylynn, who is an idiot, smoked a cigarette. Then again, I hit people with a two-by-four, so maybe I didn't have room to be a role model.

I said, "Any of you ever heard of a roller derby?"

They said they had all read the posters I put up, but no one really knew what it was.

"They have a large money prize. They skate. We skate. We could maybe get some of the other girls to join in, and we could put together a team and challenge the Darby Roller Queens when they come to town."

"We know how to skate," Sue said. "But we don't know how a roller derby works."

"I think they hit you," Raylynn said. "I think maybe I did see a movie about them once. I think they elbow you and shove you."

"I might break my nose," Gay said. "I'm too pretty to break my nose."

Coming from anyone else that would have sounded like conceit, coming from Gay it just sounded like the truth. She was in fact a work of art. We all nodded in agreement.

"Maybe we find out how it works," I said, "we could give you a minor position, Gay."

"I don't want a position."

"Sounds like a bad idea to me," Sue said. "We'd have a little over a month to get ready for that. But first, we'd have to find out what that is."

"Bob has seen them on TV," I said.

"There you are," Sue said. "Bob's seen them on TV, so we're set."

"Dot's right," Raylynn said.

We all looked at her. She still had markings on her face and under her eyes, having not quite healed up yet. She was slumped up against the wall. With those blackened eyes she looked like a raccoon lounging. She dropped her cigarette and put her heel to it.

"Who's right?" Gay said.

"My sister," Raylynn said.

"I am?" I said. "I'm right?"

"What else are we doing? Except for Gay, couple of the other girls on shifts, we're all going nowhere fast, and in a burning handbasket. I say we find out about it, train as much as possible, and do it. I say we make Dot our captain."

"I don't want my nose broke," Gay said.

"We got that," I said. "You can bring snacks."

"What we do," Raylynn said, "is we find out more about roller derby, practice, then, come August, we challenge them."

I thought: Good for you, Raylynn. Good for you.

"We'll lose," Sue said. "I don't even really know what roller derby is, but we'll lose. People like us, Gay excluded, we always lose."

"That's a nice way to look at it," I said.

"How far off am I on that?" Sue said.

"You may be on the money," Raylynn said. "But I been losing for a long time. Maybe it's time for my good number to come up. Maybe it's time for all of us to have good numbers come up."

"I'm not so sure we have numbers," Sue said.

Gay cleared her throat.

"Except for Gay," Sue said.

(12)

Raylynn's shift was slightly different from mine. She came in at the same time, but she was a year older and could work longer legally. Now and then me and Bob pushed past that, but there was a limit, only so much Bob was willing to risk, even if he paid me for that time off the books. So when I finished up for the day, I went to a café and got coffee. I could have got it at the Dairy Bob for nothing, but come quitting time I was sick of the place, and besides, Bob's coffee tasted like it was mostly made from boiling dog hair and dirt in a coffee maker. You couldn't put enough cream and sugar in it to make it taste good. The food there was decent, except for rubbery French fries, but the coffee, it was dipped straight from Hell's sewer.

I sat at a table and drank my coffee and thought about things.

Right then, in spite of what Sue had said about us not having numbers, I wanted to believe things were turning around for me. There was that whole looming court thing, of course, but there was a date Sunday with a boy who looked like a movie star, and now I had a plan to be a roller derby girl. Whatever that was.

I sat and thought about how we would split the prize money up and what I'd do with my portion. I wasn't sure what my portion was, of course, because I wasn't even sure how large a team was required for roller derby. Four? Twelve? A small army? I had no idea.

I sat there and daydreamed for several hours. The waitress, an older woman in a pink and white dress eyed me a lot, but she kept bringing coffee over. I knew how she felt. I was what they called a camper. Someone who comes in and nails down a spot and stays there drinking drinks and running the waitress. Usually, someone like that doesn't leave a tip, or much of one.

When I was ready to go, I made a point of leaving her a fair tip, and drove back to the Dairy Bob and picked up Raylynn. We then headed for the day care center to pick up the kids.

"That roller derby idea," she said. "I'm going to say it again. I'm all in."

"How come?" I said. "I thought you wouldn't like it."

Raylynn considered for a moment, said, "Last week, I wouldn't have. But now I'm looking for change. And there's the money."

"So what's up besides the money?" I asked.

Raylynn shook her head. "I guess I want to change something about myself. I guess I want to have some kind of hope that isn't tied to a man."

"Tim is a boy," I said. "He always will be."

"Boy or man," she said. "I'd like to be worth something without one or the other. I keep fastening my string to balloons that burst."

"You are worth something," I said.

"Thanks for the lie," she said.

"I was thinking of human organ sales," I said.

Raylynn almost smiled.

"What do you think about our Uncle Elbert?" I asked.

"I just met him. But he's odd. He doesn't even look like the rest of the family."

"Different mother," I said.

"I have a different father, but me and you favor a lot," she said.

"No explaining genetics," I said.

"I thought scientists did explain it," Raylynn said.

"Let me rephrase that," I said. "No way two Fender Lizards can explain it. Grandma claims he has the same nose as Dad."

"It's a nose," Raylynn said. "It looks like a lot of noses."

"Did you know he's been to prison?"

"What?"

I told her the whole story.

"And he's living in our trailer?" Raylynn said.

"Last time I looked."

"Wow," she said. "What is he? Dad's younger or older brother?"

"I think Elbert's the oldest."

"Wow," Raylynn said again. "Our very own bank robber. And he's done prison time."

"I guess I'm following in the family tradition of crime," I said.

"Look at you," Raylynn said, "all proud and stuff."

"Ha."

"Dot?"

"Yep."

"Thanks for pulling me out of that trailer. It's tight where I am now, with the kids and all of you irritating people. But I don't wake up worried every night that Tim might hit one of the babies, or me, and for no good reason at all other than the mood might strike him. Thanks, sis."

"Does this mean you're not going back?" I said.

"I think so."

"Think so?" I said.

"That's the old me talking," Raylynn said. "No. I'm not going back. I'm going to be a roller derby star. Probably with a broken leg. But I'll be a star... Well, at least I'll show up."

When I got to the house Elbert was out in the yard, and me and Sue stopped to greet him. He was sitting in a lawn chair drinking a bottle of beer, eyeing his van, which had the door slid back.

It was clean inside. Several black plastic trash bags were tied off and sitting just outside of it.

Raylynn spoke to Elbert, and he hugged her. Then she went inside the trailer. I said, "Doing a bit of house cleaning?"

"You could say that. I threw away about ninety percent of that junk. Everything was worn out. I have a little money saved up and I went to the Goodwill and bought a few things to replace them, but mostly, I'm keeping it simple."

"I see," I said.

"I got a little mattress in the van, and I'll sleep out here nights now. Raylynn and the kids need the room. Some of them can sleep in the living room if I'm out here instead of everyone jammed up in the bedrooms."

"That's nice of you," I said, and meant it.

"Yeah, well," he said. "I'll move on before long. I still got a little money left after my shopping spree, and I been thinking about picking up some day jobs to pack in a few dollars, and then I can go."

I pulled up a lawn chair. "You thinking about it or checking around?"

He grinned at me. "Mostly I'm thinking about it. Thing is, majority of people aren't big on hiring an ex-con."

"I'd hesitate to put a bank robber in my business," I said.

He nodded. "True. But I served my time. I'm out now and I'm rehabilitated. I made a decision I was going to do things straight and narrow. Come see you guys, connect with my family."

"There's that whole thing about past behavior being a pretty good indicator of future behavior," I said. "That's something Bob told me."

"This the Bob at the Dairy Bob?" Elbert asked.

"Yep."

"So he's your go to guy for philosophical thought?" Elbert asked.

"He's what I got. You see, my dad, your brother, he ran off. And I just recently met you. You kind of showed up when I was pretty much raised. So it's not like I have a lot of choices as far as male guidance goes."

"Okay. You got me there."

We sat silent for awhile. It was solid dark now and the crickets were sawing in the grass. Not far from our trailer were other trailers. They all looked pretty much alike, with their little pathetic patches of grass out front. In that moment, I can't explain it, but depression pressed against me as heavy as a big old rock.

I decided to quit thinking about it. I said, "You said you used to skate. Were you yarning me, Elbert?"

"No," he said. "I did. A lot. I made my living at it for a while."

"Skating?"

"Yes," he said. "I learned to skate when I was young, and I was good at it. Few years before I changed my career to robber, I skated at a roller rink as a clown."

"A roller skating clown?" I said. "That's priceless."

"Isn't it? But I was good. This roller rink, it was up in Kansas. How I ended up there is a long story, and I'll pass on telling that part."

"I can live with that," I said.

"So, there I was, in Kansas. And they needed someone to dress up like a clown and skate for the children, and to do children's programs."

"That must have been hard with a bottle of beer in your hand," I said.

"I am still your elder, Dot, and I've about had enough of that."

"Sorry," I said, and almost meant it.

"I skated and did skating tricks, and I was really good. And, you know, I really liked it. I seriously enjoyed it. To have the kids laugh at me was great. It was a good feeling. The money was nothing special, but it was money enough, and it was an alright job. I wish I was still doing it."

"I don't like clowns," I said. "They scare me. A skating clown might have caused me to have a heart attack."

"Fortunately," Elbert said. "Not everyone feels that way."

"Then why aren't you still skating and wearing a red nose?" I asked.

"It was a painted nose, actually," Elbert said. "If I use one of those regular clown noses, something in them breaks me out."

"Tragic if you're a clown," I said.

"Naw, I looked all right. I learned to paint myself up real good. I met this make up guy once, worked in the movies, and he showed me how to do things."

"You didn't answer me," I said. "Why did you quit the clown job?"

Elbert went quiet. Something I didn't think he could do. The expression on his face told me he was gathering up his thoughts, lining them up like soldiers.

"It was a birthday party," he said. "It was a special Saturday afternoon gig. Rich guy. His son. I guess the kid was turning eleven. There were lots of kids there. Pretty well off kids. Well, to get to it, the eleven year old boy invited a girl that was outside of the financial rodeo, so to speak. Someone, who at least from this kid's background, was poor. And black. Only black kid there.

"So, what happens is the kid comes. A pretty girl, and she doesn't bring a present. I don't know. Forgot. Didn't have the money. I don't know. No big deal to the boy. He was glad to see her. It was pretty clear to me he had a kind of sweet crush on that lovely little girl. But the dad didn't like it. I think he didn't like his lily-white son being with someone from across the tracks, someone black. He started criticizing the girl for not bringing a present. Kind of joking, but mean joking, and she got her feelings hurt, which was understandable, and went off crying. The rich man's son was devastated. He skated after the girl, who had reached the edge of the rink and was unfastening her skates. The father tried to stop him, and I stopped the father."

"Stopped how?" I asked.

"I just meant to touch his shoulder," Elbert said. "You know, get his attention. Say something like, 'Hey, man. It's okay. Let him go.' Didn't work that way."

"How did it work?" I asked.

"When he turned around to see who had him, saw me in my clown get-up, he just freaked out. Said to get my hand off of him. He'd decide who his son should chase and shouldn't, and then he said something that went all over me. He called her the N word, as they say now days.

"I hit him, Dot. I hit him so hard it seemed to me the lights in the building dimmed. He went down like a dead tree falling.

Unconscious. When I looked up, all those kids at the party were looking at me. The clown had cold-cocked the father of the birthday boy."

"He had it coming," I said.

Elbert shook his head. "He had it coming. But that doesn't mean I should have done it. Traumatic stuff. You come to a birthday party and the hired clown on roller skates knocks the birthday boy's father on his ass. It didn't make the situation better, me trying to stand up for the girl, it made it worse. I skated out of there and went home, and the next day I got an assault charge slapped on me. I deserved it. He said something rotten about that little girl. He was a jerk. But he didn't try and hurt me physically, and I hit him. An impulsive thing. I felt good about it for about fifteen minutes, and then all I could think about was what if he had hit his head real hard on the floor things could have gone real wrong real quick? I thought about all those kids seeing me doing it. That's an image they have for ever. Bozo the Clown goes rogue."

"Are you trying to tell me something, Elbert?" I said. "Maybe something you've already told me?"

"Telling something once has never stopped me from telling it again," Elbert said.

"I believe that," I said.

"I'm saying it made me feel good in the moment. He had it coming. But it was a bad move. I did a couple days in jail, and finally got someone I knew to go my bail. What I'm saying is you did something where someone deserved it a lot more than my rich fella deserved it. He was just a jerk. Raylynn's boyfriend was beating on her. But it still doesn't make it right. A temper like that, you got to get hold of it. You can do more damage than you can ever imagine, no matter how right you are."

"All right," I said. "I get it."

"I'm not trying to tell you how to run your life," Elbert said. "But I'm trying to tell you some of the stupid things I did that could be a lot like stupid things you might do. Or have done."

"You're saying do as you say, not as you did?" I said.

"Yeah," he said with a nod. "I'm also saying I've learned from my mistakes. Or I've tried to."

"What happened to the birthday boy and the girl?" I asked.

"I don't know. I never saw any of them again," he said.

We sat there in our lawn chairs with the night all around us, the stars up above. Just listening to the crickets work. It was a comfortable night. The summer having given up some of its heat to a bit of cool wind down from the North. I didn't mention to Elbert that I had already passed on his bit of wisdom to Sue, and that he was talking to the converted. Well. The almost converted.

(14)

I went in to see the judge, and it was different than I thought. It was just a little room in the courthouse. The judge, an older woman with red hair out of a bottle and a look on her face that made you think she had just bitten into an unripe persimmon, sat behind a long table with some plastic chairs pulled up to it. She wasn't wearing a judge robe like I thought she'd be. She had on a green pantsuit. She was sitting in one of the plastic chairs, and there was a little, bald man in a black suit and white shirt and no tie, sitting in a chair near her recording all of it on a machine.

There was a big bailiff down front near the table. He had a huge belly that pushed at his uniform, a shaved head, and enough fat on the back of his neck it had coiled there like a snake. His face was red and sweaty, even though it was air conditioned in the room. He had the kind of face that would have looked tired while sleeping, looked like at any moment he might blow a major hose.

There were metal fold-out chairs out front of the table, and they were arranged so that they were divided in the middle, making a kind of hallway between them that led to the door.

On my side of the room in the front row were Grandma, actually sitting in two chairs (If I'm lying, I'm dying). And there was Mom, Raylynn and Elbert, also sitting in the front row. Bob was there too. He had left Sue in charge of the Dairy Bob. He looked a little nervous, like he was thinking, meanwhile, back at the Dairy Bob the monkeys have taken over the zoo.

I was sitting up front beside Bob.

Tim came in. He had a lawyer. A guy that looked as if he had been on a six day drunk and had been angrily awake about five minutes. Bob leaned over, said, "Jim Cubert. A real ambulance chaser."

We all had to stand up and face the judge. Some formal stuff was said by the bailiff, and then the judge motioned me and Tim and his lawyer up front and everyone else was told to sit down. She said to me, "Do you have a lawyer?"

"No, ma'am," I said. "I couldn't afford one."

"The court can appoint you one, you know?" she said.

"No, ma'am. I didn't know."

"Well, you can have one if you like, but I don't think it's necessary."

I probably should have said then that I wanted a lawyer anyway, but I didn't. I was nervous and really wasn't thinking straight.

I looked over at Tim. He was a little rough looking from my going over him with the board, but he looked healthy enough, if maybe a little drunk, like his lawyer.

"Tell me what happened," the judge said to Tim.

"I was coming home at night," he said, "and this psycho jumped me from behind and hit me with a board. She knocked me out and left me in the yard."

The judge looked at his lawyer, said, "Does counsel have anything to add?"

"Not at this moment," the lawyer said.

The judge studied Tim for a long moment, then turned to me. "All right, Miss. Tell your side."

"He was beating on my sister, and she was pretty bad off. Marked up and the like. I sat out in the yard under a tree with a two-by-four and waited for him to come home. I came up behind him and whacked him with the board some. I was afraid for my sister's life. I was afraid he might hurt her bad. It wasn't the first time he hit her."

"Did you hit him hard?" the judge asked.

"I figured if I was going to hit him," I said, "I might as well not waste my energy, so I went for the whole hog."

The judge nodded, looked at Tim. "Did you hit your wife?"

"No, ma'am," he said. "Not guilty."

"I didn't ask if you were guilty or not guilty. I asked if you hit your wife."

"No, ma'am," he said.

"Liar," I said. "Liar, liar, pants on fire."

The judge smiled at me. "We're not in the school yard, young lady."

"Sorry," I said. "It just came out."

"Do you have proof he hit his wife?" the judge asked me.

"I have his wife here," I said. "My sister."

I turned and pointed at her.

"Stand up," the judge said to Raylynn.

Raylynn stood. She still had a darkened face where Tim had hit her. The judge said, "Did this boy hit you?"

"Yes, ma'am," Raylynn said.

"More than once?" the judge said.

"Lots of times in lots of places," Raylynn said. "More than once on more than one occasion. I was scared he'd hit the kids. Well, he did hit them some."

"How many kids?" the judge asked.

"Two," Raylynn said.

"Are you married to this gentleman?" the judge asked.

"No," Raylynn said. "We live together. Or did."

"Is he the father of either of the children?" the judge asked.

"One of them," Raylynn said.

"You know what's causing that, right?" the judge said.

"Ma'am," Raylynn said.

"You getting pregnant," the judge said. "You know what's causing that?"

Raylynn was slightly caught off guard. She finally said, "Yes, ma'am."

"Just checking," the judge said. "And the children were home when this alleged striking of your person took place?"

"Nothing alleged about it," my mother said.

"You don't talk," the judge said.

My mother, dressed in a polka-dot dress that made her look like some kind of spotted wild animal, said, "Sorry."

The judge leaned back in her chair and studied Tim. She looked at me. She looked at Raylynn. She looked at the ceiling. She looked back at Tim.

"You're a big strapping lad," the judge said. "You shouldn't be hitting women."

"I didn't," Tim said.

"I think you're a liar," the judge said.

"Objection," the lawyer said.

"Shut up, Jim," the judge said.

"That's not right," Jim said. "There's a rule of law."

"Yeah," the judge said, "and I'm going to save the court and everybody a lot of time by going around it. I think your client hit the girl. I think that makes him a scumbag in my book."

"This is out of order," the lawyer said.

"Last time I tell you to shut up," the judge said.

The lawyer went silent, found a spot on the wall to look at.

"Here's what I see," the judge said. "Folks on this girl's side of the room. Including a sister who looks like she's a lot worse off than this boy as far as a beating goes. But I don't see anyone on this boy's side of the room, besides you, Jim. And to tell you the truth, I don't consider that a high recommendation."

"That's not fair, judge," the lawyer said.

"Life is just full of unfairness," she said. "Here's my ruling. You, son, are going to drop all charges, because I think you're a bully and a creep. I think that because you have come into my court and you've been drinking, and your lawyer has been drinking. Six feet away your breath is curling the hair on the back of my neck."

"Judge," the lawyer said, "you can't just decide we've been drinking."

"I can get a breathalyzer and make this even worse for the two of you, or you can accept what I say. Tell me out loud. Have you been drinking? And if you say no, then we bring in a breathalyzer."

The lawyer cleared his throat. "I had a little nip with breakfast."

The judge looked at Tim.

"I reckon I had a little nip at breakfast too."

"Were the two of you together when you had this little nip?" the judge asked.

They nodded.

"Uh-huh. Here's how it is. Charges are dropped. But," and she turned her attention to me. "Young lady, much as I despise a man that will strike a woman, you really can't go around sneaking up on people with a board. Even if they are a coward and a bully and a liar. Hear me?"

"Yes, ma'am," I said.

"I'm going to give you a stretch of probation," she said. "A week where every morning you go out to the Marvel Creek Dog Rescue and clean up after the dogs."

"But I have a job," I said.

"That does present a problem," the judge said. "But, it's not my problem. You be there. One week. Two hours every morning. Ten to noon. Understood?"

"Yes, ma'am," I said.

Tim's lawyer cleared his throat.

"Yes," the judge said.

"What about parental rights?" the lawyer said.

"What about them," the judge said.

"Tim should have the right to visit his child," he said.

"I'm going to rule no for awhile," the judge said. "Until his girlfriend heals up, then you can come back to court and we'll see what we can arrange. In the meantime, young man, don't go near this lady. You hear?"

"Yes, ma'am," Tim said.

"You do," the judge said, "you may find yourself wearing a nice orange jumpsuit provided by the county. Got me?"

"Yes, ma'am," Tim said.

"Good," said the judge, and not having a gavel, slapped her hand on the table. "Court adjourned." She got up. The court reporter who was recording it all got up and tucked the machine under his arm. He and the judge went out together. Tim and his drunk lawyer went out quickly, not looking at anyone.

The bailiff sighed like he was taking his last breath, and went out. The rest of us waited a moment, and then we left.

I went out mornings to the Marvel Creek Dog Rescue and scooped up dog poop in the concrete runs with a little lidded shovel on a long handle.

The runs had fencing on the sides, and on one end the runs went into a large building. On the other end they went outside. The runs were long, and they opened at both ends with a gate. The gate at the back emptied out into a hundred fenced acres spotted with trees and a small pond. All of that was surrounded by a high chain-link fence.

Sometimes the dogs were let loose out there, though not necessarily altogether. Some of the dogs got along well, some didn't.

I was taught not only to scoop poop, which was really not a part of the job that required great instruction, but when and which dogs to let out in the open, how to feed them, groom them, and so on. By the fourth day I had some idea of what was going on.

There were all manner of dogs out there, all rescue dogs. Dogs that had been abused, abandoned, or had been put there when their masters died. Puppies born to strays. No dog that lived there was put down due to convenience, but since there was a constant stream of animals, the reserve could only hold so many.

I fed them and watered them. I spent time with them. I petted them. All of the dogs were friendly. Even the ones that looked kind of scary, like the pit bulls and the Dobermans. What they wanted was what I guess everyone wanted. Attention. Love. A place to stay.

I felt like they were my peeps.

The lady who ran the shelter was called High Top for some reason I didn't know. She was a lean woman, brown from the sun, probably too much sun. Her hair was long and nearly white, but I figured she wasn't any more than in her mid-thirties. She was pretty in a sun-damaged kind of way. She always wore tee-shirts and shorts and black work shoes with white socks that went to her knees. Her long hair was gathered in the back with a black hair clamp.

"You're good at this," she said.

I was closing up a cage when she walked up.

"Thanks."

"You're a natural for dealing with dogs."

"I didn't actually have a choice," I said.

"I get that," High Top said, "but that doesn't change the fact you're good at it. Maybe you might want a job here."

"One that pays?"

"We don't pay much," she said, "and we run through employees frequently. All the scooping of dog poop gets to them. But we can pay you all right. It's a good job for someone preparing for college."

"But I'm not," I said.

"That's hard to believe," she said.

That caught me off guard. "Why's that?"

"You seem like a college kid," she said. "I just assumed you were going to college."

"I'm here on probation," I said. "You get many kids from college on probation?"

"More than you would think," she said. "Mostly kids like you that did something stupid, but fortunately, nothing major."

"Well," I said. "I'm not a college kid. I don't even have my high school diploma."

"You can go back to school," she said.

"I thought I'd take my GED," I said. "I keep meaning to do it."

"Meaning to doesn't get it done," High Top said.

"It's hard to do and work," I said.

"What I did," High Top said.

"Really?" I was surprised. I thought the GED was just for trailer trash like myself.

"Really," High Top said. "I took the GED then went to A&M University. I got a degree in veterinary medicine, but what I ended up doing was putting together this refuge."

"Was it hard to do?" I asked.

"Oh, yeah. I had to find donors. Sometimes the place does fine, at other times not so much. I've been on the edge of closing several times."

"What would happen to the dogs if you closed?" I asked.

Her face soured. "For those I couldn't find homes, which of course is always the goal...I place a lot of pets... But for those I couldn't find homes, they would go to the local animal shelter, and a large percentage of them would be put down."

"That's terrible," I said.

High Top nodded. "It is. But that's what happens to a large number of the dogs they can't find homes for. Bad as it sounds, they don't really have a choice. Here, I'm trying to do something different. I work at full capacity all the time. I place a dog, another one comes in. One dies—and sadly it happens—another comes in. There's not a single empty run here. I feed them well. I let them run inside a fenced compound. They have a safe place at night. I know each and every one of them, and pet them all. You're welcome to pet as many as you can."

"Do you get any bad dogs?"

"Now and again," she said. "Mostly bad dogs wouldn't be that way if they hadn't been treated badly. Bad lives make bad animals. For that matter, bad lives make bad people."

High Top paused and looked down the row of kennels.

"You know what I like about these dogs?" she asked.

"They don't judge you?" I said.

She turned to me and smiled. "Exactly. And they're always happy to see me. I like all animals, but dogs, they're special. Some people are dog people. Some are cat people. Have you heard the old joke about what the main difference is between cats and dogs?"

I shook my head.

"A dog thinks: My owner feeds me, houses me, pets me, takes care of me, therefore, the owner must be god. The cat thinks: My owner feeds me, houses me, pets me, takes care of me, therefore I must be god."

I laughed.

"Dogs," she said. "There's something about that love they have that surpasses most anything. They can help you find a place in yourself that's really nice. That's what I like best about them. They do more for me than I can ever do for them."

"Well, I guess I better finish up," I said.

"Sure," High Top said. "You think about that job offer."

"Okay."

"And the GED," she said. "I'll help you prepare for it, if you like."

"Sure," I said. Thinking I might never actually get around to it.

High Top walked off and I went back to work.

(16)

On Sunday, when I finished up with the dogs, I drove home and started getting ready for my date. I didn't know exactly how to get ready for a real date, since I'd never had a really good one. I'd gone to the movies with a boy a few times, but it was with other people too, and maybe it was a date of sorts, but it didn't feel like one. It felt like a communal get together. We had fun at the movie, and when it was over the boy I was with and the other boys poked each other and giggled, and played grab ass with each other, and we all went home. I found the whole event about as exciting as watching an ant crawl.

I picked out different wardrobes, but there wasn't anything that jumped out at me. I really didn't know what to wear. I wasn't sure where we were going. Herb said some place nice to eat. Maybe a movie. I didn't want to underdress, but I didn't want to overdress either. I tried a cute top with blue jeans, and thought that looked all right. But maybe on a first date, going to some place fancy, Herb sporting me around, I should wear something a little nicer. And then again, who said the place would be fancy? He said nice.

I tried on several dresses, but thought all of them looked funny on me. I had worn them before and felt they looked all right then, but suddenly they didn't look the same way. I couldn't decide if it was the dresses that were wrong, or if I was in a mood. Or both.

I sat down on the bed and thought about shoes. I thought about buying a new outfit, but I didn't really have the money for that.

Grandma came into the room. And bless her, when she walked in wearing that big colorful dress, she looked like a circus tent being shoved by the wind. She looked at all the clothes I had spread out on my bed.

"You taking that stuff to the Goodwill?"

"No," I said.

"She has a date," Mama said. She was standing at the bedroom doorway, looking in. I hadn't told her or anyone I had a date.

"A date?" Grandma said, as if me going on a real date was the strangest thing, next in oddness only to aliens landing in a saucer on the White House lawn and insisting they show the first lady how to cook an omelet.

"I noticed it right off," Mama said coming into the room, sitting on the edge of the bed. "She has that blank stare about her."

"She's not old enough to date," Grandma said.

"She certainly is," Mama said. "I was married when I was just a year older than her."

"And how did that work out?" Grandma said.

"Not well," Mama said. "But this isn't about marriage, it's about a date."

"One leads to the other," Grandma said, and sat on the bed. I could feel it shift, like a raft trying to ferry an elephant across a river.

"You pick out something yet?" Mama asked.

"No," I said.

"What kind of date is it?"

I told her what I knew.

"Here's a thought," Mama said. "A simple black dress with nice flat shoes. No high heels. That's a little too glitzy, I think, and the damn things will hurt your feet."

"Here's another thought," Grandma said. "Stay home. Boys are terrible people. Just look at your father."

She had a point. But I kept thinking about Herb and how he looked and how nice he had been.

"I don't have a simple black dress," I said. "I have a simple somewhat gray dress that was once black but has faded and has what might be a permanent chili stain next to the neckline."

"I got a little money," Mama said. "You ought to have a dress. You go down town and buy you something."

"We can't afford that," I said.

"Sure we can," she said. "I'll get the money, and you go shopping. Maybe it's best you drive over to Tyler, where they got a good mall. You go over there and see what they got. What I can give you isn't much money, but it's something. Maybe you could put it with anything you have saved up."

"All right," I said. "Thanks."

"The other thing I want," Mama said, "is I want you to have fun. You don't have a lot of fun. You're the age when you should be having fun. You work, hit people with a board, and scoop up dog crap. You should be having fun."

"Did you have fun at my age, Mama?" I asked.

"No," she said.

"Me neither," grandma said.

"Why?"

"We both got married too early, and we both got married to men we shouldn't have married."

"At least my husband died young," Grandma said to Mama. "He didn't run off."

"Thanks," Mama said. "That makes me feel a lot better."

"I'm not trying to make you feel better," Grandma said.

"I guessed that," Mama said. She looked at me. "Come on, Dot. Let me get you that money."

(17)

Mama gave me the money and I got my wallet and stuck it in my back pocket. I hate carrying a purse for the most part, and try not to. I started out to my car. Elbert was sitting in a lawn chair again. It was past noon and it was hot and he was sweating. His face looked like it had been sugar-glazed. He glanced at me as I went by.

"You going to work?" he asked.

"No," I said. "Sunday I'm off from the Dairy Bob, and I've done the dog duty. How about you? You going to work? Ever?"

"I'm looking for opportunities," he said.

"You job hunting with mental telepathy?" I asked.

About that time my little brother, Frank, came out of the trailer. "She's got a date. I was listening."

I looked at Frank. "Thanks, Frank. Smooth. You little eavesdropper."

"I ain't no eye dropper," Frank said.

"Eavesdropper," I said. "Forget it."

Frank pretty much had forgot it. He pulled his bike out from under the trailer, which was up about three feet on blocks, got on it and rode off. As he went, he looked back and grinned at me.

"I guess it's not classy to hit your little brother with a board," I said.

Elbert ignored that, said, "You got a date, huh?"

"You know, Elbert, it's not really any of your business."

"Do you know him well?"

"We just met," I said. "At the Dairy Bob. And I told you, it isn't any of your business."

"You ought to know more about him before you go out with him, Dot."

"Most likely, to know more about him, I have to go out with him," I said.

"But you got to be careful about it," Elbert said. "You got to keep in mind that boys have a kind of single-minded view at that age."

"Are you about to give me a lesson on the birds and the bees?" I said.

"I'm pretty sure you know about the birds and the bees," Elbert said. "And you're smart, and you're wary, but I think you want attention bad enough to let down your guard."

"Attention?" I said. "I get plenty of attention."

"A boy might seem like a knight in shining armor. But you're young, Dot. You got a lot ahead of you."

"We're not planning a wedding," I said. "We're going on a date."

"I'm just saying—"

"Well don't say," I said. "Don't say anything. You're not my father."

"I know," Elbert said. "But since he's gone—"

"Since he's gone nothing," I said. "You aren't anything to me. What you are is a middle-aged man I just met recently living in a van in our front yard. And you were a skating clown for heaven's sake. I don't need advice from you."

"I was just trying to help, Dot."

"Don't," I said, and climbed in my car and drove away.

I had only driven about a block when I felt bad about how angry I was, and wondered just why I was so angry. Was it because he had nailed me exactly as I was? Or was it because my entire family saw men as creeps?

I drove over to Tyler. It was about an hour and a half drive. I was watching the time close. I had to find something to wear, drive back home, get dressed, and be ready by eight. I had it planned so he would pick me up at the Dairy Bob. I was kind of ashamed of myself, but I didn't want him to see that run down trailer, or have to navigate Elbert and his van parked in the yard.

I looked around the mall and found something right off, which I didn't expect, and it was on sale. I tried it on and it fit just the way I wanted it to. I looked myself over in the mirror and thought I looked pretty dang good.

It was as Mama suggested, a little black dress, and I bought some good shoes, not heels, and I knew I had a bit of jewelry at the house that could set the whole thing off. I might not knock him dead, but with my hair washed and brushed out, I might at least startle him a bit, like walking up on a preoccupied bunny.

I was so happy with what I bought, I drove over to On The Border, which was not far from the store where I bought my goods, and ordered myself a Mexican lunch, one of the cheaper specials. Except for the Dairy Bob, and a cup of coffee and maybe some pie at the local café, it was rare I ever ate out. It was rare the family ate out.

It came pretty quick, and while I was eating an enchilada I realized I was also eating out tonight and that Mexican food might swell me up in my dress like a sausage. I ended up eating just a little bit, and having the rest boxed up. I knew that once it went into the refrigerator at home, I'd probably never see it again. Either Elbert or Frank or Grandma would pounce on it like a duck on a June bug.

I paid up and went home.

(18)

I was dressed at seven-forty-five, and rushed out to the car to head for the Dairy Bob.

Of course, Elbert, who seemed to be constantly camped outside, saw me coming out. It was still light out, the way it is that time of year in East Texas, so I got a good look at him, and he got a good look at me.

"You look nice," he said. "Probably too nice for the likes of whoever."

"Thanks," I said. "I think."

I drove to the Dairy Bob, and when I got there I parked out back, the way me and Herb had arranged, and waited. After a few minutes I decided he had stood me up.

I looked at my watch. It was eight on the dot. Okay. Impatient much?

Right at that moment, Herb pulled up in his very nice and expensive red convertible beside me. The car looked as bright and shiny as a saucer fresh-licked by a cat. His car made me feel as if I was sitting in a donkey cart and the donkey was dead. I got out and walked over. Herb stepped out, went around and opened the door for me.

The only time anyone opened the door ahead of me like that was my brother Frank, who was pushing to get past me.

"Thank you," I said. "But you don't need to do that. I can open the door."

"Call it a gesture of politeness, this being a first date," Herb said.

"So," I said, as I got in, "on the second date you were planning to drop this part of the action anyway?"

"Pretty much," he said, and grinned at me. "Man, you look terrific."

"Thanks," I said. "I didn't know if I was overdressing or underdressing."

"You are dressed for anything. Do you have a curfew?"

I didn't, but I wanted to play it safe. I said, "Midnight."

"Okay," he said. "I thought we could go to the Gabardine."

"That's a nice place," I said.

"For this small town, yeah," he said, and that made me realize that Herb knew a lot more about life, good restaurants and bad, than I did. I knew without him saying it that he had spent summers in Europe.

"Or," he said, "we can go to the movies, have a hot dog and popcorn."

"Nope. I have a nice dress on. I'm all up for a nice place."

The Gabardine is the only truly nice restaurant in our town. It's on the side opposite of the Dairy Bob, and where I live. It's on the side where there are no trailers and no cars up on blocks and no overturned washing machines in the yard. It's on the side of town where women get their nails done by other people, and not with just an emery board and nail polish. It's the side of town where people have time to do things besides work. It's the side of town that smells like money. It's the kind of place that made me wish I'd worn high heels. It's on a tall hill that over looks the highway. Herb drove us up there and opened my door and helped me out.

Herb gave the key to a man in a red jacket, and the man drove the car away. I had seen valet service in the movies, but never in real life.

Inside there were glass fish tanks. They were full of bright, swimming fish. A man greeted Herb by name, directed us to a table by a window that looked out over a pond made of rocks and colored cement. There were stripped and spotted fish in the pond.

"You had reservations?" I said, as Herb held out my chair for me to sit. "You knew I'd come here?"

"I have a standing reservation," he said. "If I come, they find me a table. If I don't, then, no problem. That sounded kind of elitist, didn't it?"

"A little."

"My parents own part of the restaurant. They are investors with the Gabardines. And, for the record the Gabardines are my grandparents on my mother's side."

"Oh," I said.

I looked at the menu. The cheapest thing on it was the price of one whole side of the Dairy Bob menu, counting the waitress's wages and a tip, maybe the insurance on the building. I looked around for something cheap, and then thought, what the heck. His folks own part of the restaurant, and I am on a date, and he wants to impress me, and I want a steak.

When the waiter came, I ordered a filet mignon with all the trimmings. Herb didn't blink an eye. Even so, I felt kind of guilty. Maybe I'd skip dessert.

I didn't, though. I had a slice of chocolate cake that was so rich in chocolate and sugar it made my head swim like those fish in the aquarium. I was glad I had skipped eating all the Mexican food earlier. I hoped after eating I didn't look too porky in my little black dress.

When we finished, Herb ordered coffee. It was rich and tasty and the cream in it was real, not out of a little package you had to peel open yourself. I had never had coffee that good. Frankly, I had never had a meal that good. My mother was a mediocre cook, and my grandmother thought warming up a TV dinner was really putting on the dog. I didn't like to think a steak, a cake, and a cup of coffee could impress me that much, but it did.

Herb sipped his coffee, smiled at me. If you could bottle that smile you'd be a millionaire.

"So," Herb said, "where exactly do you live?"

I hesitated, but came out with it anyway. "In a trailer on the other side of town, out in Judge Park."

"I don't know where that is," he said.

"I'm not surprised," I said. "There's no reason for you to know."

"What's that mean?"

"It means you have money. You have a very different life… Ah, heck. I'm starting to turn this into something I didn't mean to."

"No, that's all right," he said, reaching out and touching my hand briefly. "I want to know."

"If you have money, you have no reason to know about my side of town. I live with my mother, my grandmother, and my little brother. Recently, there's also my sister and her two kids, and I shouldn't fail to mention I have an uncle who lives on the yard in a van."

"The yard?"

"He just showed up one day. None of us had ever seen him before. I might add I didn't list my father in that group. He went out for a pack of cigarettes a few years ago, and didn't come back. Your turn."

"Boring. I live on Frank Street. It's—"

"I know where it is," I said. "Point I was making. I know where you live. Know the name of the street, but who the hell has heard of Judge Park unless you live there? Sorry. I was asking about you."

He grinned at me. "You have a lot to say."

"Sorry."

"No. I like it."

"You do?"

"Sure," he said. "All the girls I know are very proper."

"Oh, thanks."

"That's not what I meant," he said. "I meant you speak your mind. You have opinions. I don't know which ones I agree with yet, but at least you have them. In answer to your question, my mother has a nice dress shop in Tyler. My father has an office downtown. He really doesn't do much, and he doesn't go there often. But he has a title. My mother runs the shop at a loss as a hobby. My father plays a lot of golf. They have investments, like this restaurant. Nothing exciting. But they're okay. They've done all right by me. They didn't choose to be boring, and they didn't plan on being rich. They inherited a lot of money. Like I said, boring."

"You're complaining?" I said.

"No. I'm just saying it lacks challenges."

"Sounds nice," I said. "But challenges can be highly overrated. At least you don't get up every day wondering if there will be what the electric and water company like to call an interruption in service. When my dad left, I inherited a few comic books and some empty cigarette wrappers and fifty-two cents he left in an ash tray. And you want to know the worst part?"

"What?"

"The comics he left, none of them are that good. And I've long ago spent the fifty-two cents."

*O**ddly, I hadn't noticed** how beautiful the night really was.* Not in a long while. I always seemed to be darting through it, from trailer to car, from car to the Dairy Bob. But after we came out of the restaurant, I looked up. Sometimes there's too much light in town to see the sky well, but here in the parking lot, perhaps designed to be more romantic, there were fewer lights and the night was clear. The sky was a soft black stretch of forever with endless diamonds thrown against it, winking down at us. The air was sweet as honey.

When we were in the car, Herb said, "It's a nice night. Want to take a drive?"

"Sure," I said. "A drive sounds nice."

He drove us through town, out past the Dairy Bob, along the highway, and past the city limits. I don't know what I was feeling then, not really. Knowing only I was in the car with a handsome young man and that we were away from prying eyes, and that it was a beautiful night, and I was full of a lovely dinner. Things got even better when Herb lowered the top on the convertible and my hair lifted in the wind. I had spent some time brushing it and shaping it, and there was part of me that didn't like all that work to go to waste, but the other part of me loved the idea of the wind in my hair.

The houses fell away and the trees sprang up and the highway climbed. There aren't a lot of truly high places in East Texas, and a big hill to us is a mountain. I recognized the area we were approaching as we came closer to it, and my throat tightened like someone had glued its sides together.

It was Outlander's Drop. I don't know how it came by that name, but that was what it was called by older folks thereabouts, but the kids called it Lover's Drop, a place between Marvel Creek and not a place not too far away called Camp Rapture.

We pulled off the highway and down a little dirt road toward the edge of Outlander's Drop. It was mostly clear up there, so it wasn't like it was in the deep forests. There was only one lightning split tree up on the hill, and we pulled up in front of that split and parked. When Herb cut the engines the inside lights on the dash went black. It seemed as if all the world had gone silent.

I thought of something my sister, Raylynn had told me. About how this was where it had happened. Where her first boyfriend and her had made her first child. In that moment, looking through that lightning split tree, the stars I could see no longer were lovely, but were more like cheap costume jewelry tossed on a dark and dirty sheet.

"Pretty, isn't it?" Herb said.

I started to say something, but the words got fat in my mouth and I couldn't get them out.

Herb reached over and touched my hand on the seat between us. He took hold of it gently. I felt something in my stomach move around and then I jerked my hand away, opened the car door and got out. I held the door open, like that mattered. With the top down it was easy to talk to him.

"Go home, Herb. It isn't going to happen."

"What?"

"You aren't going to get what you think you were. You may have money, and I may be white trash, but don't think that makes you so special I'll just fold for you."

"What?"

"You said that," I said, and closed the door. I walked over and stood on the edge of the Drop. It was pretty high. It went down at a slant. Below I could see brush in the moonlight, and when a thin cloud rolled over the moon, it changed the light down there and the brush seemed to move. It made a chill run up my back.

Herb was out of the car. He came up beside me. He said, "I don't know what you thought, but—"

"Save it for someone stupid," I said, and started walking.

I went around the car and down the road as fast as I could go in my nice new shoes, feeling silly as a cartoon character in my little black dress. The dreams in my head were coming apart like cotton candy.

"Dot," Herb said. "Come back. Come get in the car. We can leave."

I kept walking.

I walked along the road and thought it was sure a long ways. I was going to be able to make it into town about the time I turned thirty-five.

Herb pulled up beside me, driving slowly. "Come on, Dot. I didn't mean to offend you. I just took your hand."

"Yeah, but my hand is attached to the rest of me," I said as I walked.

"I don't know what you thought, but you're wrong."

I kept walking. He kept cruising beside me.

"I didn't mean to offend you in any kind of way," he said. "Hand holding isn't exactly criminal. Did you hate my touching your hand all that much?"

The gravel on the road crunched as the car glided alongside me.

"I liked it too much," I said. "I didn't want to get too deep in the dream, and more importantly, I don't want two kids and a run away father, and me living in a trailer with dirty diapers, wearing a muumuu."

"A what?"

"Never mind."

"Dot, at least get in the car and let me take you home. It's at least ten miles into town."

I kept walking, wanting to make a point. But after a few more steps I thought ten miles was indeed pretty far.

I quit walking. Herb stopped the car.

"I won't touch your hand," he said, "or any other part of your anatomy. We can discuss politics. We can talk about the rising prices of farm-raised chicken. I don't care. I won't leave you out here by yourself. I'll drive alongside you all the way home if I have to."

I got in the car.

I guess we drove for five minutes without speaking. I glanced at Herb out of the corner of my eye. He looked like his insides had collapsed.

I said, "I'm sorry."

"What?"

"I said I'm sorry. Don't make me say it again."

"I'm not making you say it at all," he said.

"I… It's hard to explain."

"I think we have a little time if you'd like to try," he said.

"I don't want to."

"So I'm just going to have this mystery?"

I was silent for awhile before I spoke. "I read more into that than you meant. Or maybe I read into it what I meant. I like you. I'm attracted to you. I felt like if I didn't get out of the car right then I might go where I shouldn't."

"I wasn't trying to—" He paused. "Well, I guess it could lead to that. That's natural."

"Yeah, and we both know what that means," I said.

"It's not a bad thing unto itself…I think we're talking about the same thing."

"No, it isn't," I said. "And yes, we are talking about the same thing… You meant sex, right?"

"Yep."

"Okay," I said. "Just checking. It's the timing that's bad. My sister could tell you a little about timing. This thing we're talking about has to mean more than a good dinner and a nice drive under the stars."

"I just wanted to hold your hand and talk," Herb said. "I think I might have wanted a kiss too. That part could have waited until I took you home."

"I overreacted," I said. "I felt like a hole had opened up under me and I was falling in. It may not be an excuse for how I acted, but my sister has two kids, and neither by Immaculate Conception. Two fathers, two kids, and they both are out of the picture, and one of them I beat with a two-by-four. I know I've told you this, but there it is again."

"Not the two-by-four part," he said.

"We'll save that for later," I said. "And I'll just say again my father ran off and didn't even leave us with a pack of chewing gum. Not a word since."

"You had mentioned that before," Herb said, "but the chewing gum part is new. You ever think maybe something happened to him."

"Now and then," I said. "All I know is I want something better. You follow me?"

"I do. I get it. But I still don't think holding your hand is going to cause you to wear a muumuu."

"Hand holding has its repercussions, you know."

He smiled. "Friends?"

"Sure," I said. We drove on, and long before we got back to town, and the lights became too bright, and everything turned too familiar, and oh so real, for a long, good moment the stars once again looked nice up there and the wind was sweet as honey.

(20)

He didn't take me straight to my car, and that's because I asked him not to. When I did that, he looked at me sideways, but didn't argue. He said, "Where to?"

I told him I wanted coffee, and I wanted it in the coffee shop where I had gone to wait on Raylynn.

There was hardly anyone there, just an older guy at a back booth with a cup of coffee, reading a newspaper.

Herb ordered coffee and pie. I ordered coffee. I wanted the pie, but after that cake I had I held back. Not only for the waistline, but because I thought it might have been making me loopy. Sweets do that to me. I had treated Herb like he was a rapist, rather than a young man with normal appetites. Actually, it was my own appetites I was afraid of. And I didn't just mean a craving for pie.

We talked, and Herb said, "You seem to think poor people are less happy than rich people."

"Did I say that?"

"No," he said. "But you implied it."

"Well, I think being unhappy with money might be better than being unhappy without it."

"Unhappy is pretty much unhappy," Herb said. "Even if you can afford to feel bad in a nice car and a house with an ocean view you still feel bad."

"I suppose," I said.

"My family is happy," he said. "A little boring, as I said, but happy. They made me happy. Money helped, I'm sure. But that's not it. My parents love each other. That's it. Bottom line."

"My parents loved each other too, but that didn't work out," I said. "Maybe money pressure had something to do with that."

"Maybe it was pressure of character," he said.

"What's that supposed to mean?"

"Wait a moment now," he said. "I'm not trying to make you bristle. What I'm saying is character is what you do when you don't have to. And though my parents have money, I've seen their character tested. They came out all right."

"Yeah, well, my dad came out on the other side somewhere, and I don't know if he got the cigarettes or not. But I guess the rest of us are all right."

Herb grinned at me. "All I'm saying is don't think everything's easy for me because I have money. Which is not to say I don't have some advantages."

"You're going to college, I'm studying to take a GED," I said. "Or, I should be."

"And you'll pass it. And you'll move on."

My insecurity slipped out. "You think so?"

"Sure. You're bright. I love talking to you. Everything isn't about cars and dresses and parties."

"Because I can't afford cars and dresses and parties," I said.

"I don't think that's it," he said.

"I didn't make you mad earlier?"

"You surprised me," he said. "Embarrassed me a little."

"I'm sorry."

"Don't be, Dot. It's all right."

The waitress, a different one than I had before, filled our cups and took away Herb's empty pie plate. We sat there awhile, and then we went to the bowling alley, and bowled. I was terrible at it. But Herb was worse. I thought once he might not be able to get his fingers out of the ball. It looked like he might go down the alley with it.

When we finished bowling he took me to my car and followed me home. Elbert was sitting in his chair out in the yard. I got out of my car, and climbed into Herb's car and sat beside him.

"Is that your uncle?"

"Yep, that's him," I said. "Hey, I'm sorry I was a jackass." I reached over and took his hand. "See. I don't think you're going to attack me. I like you."

"I like you too."

"Enough to see me again?" I asked. "I can bring a straight jacket and you can have me wear it. I won't mind."

"You're fine the way you are," he said.

I looked through the windshield. Elbert was moving from side to side in his chair to see what was going on in the car.

I said, "I'd love to kiss you. Really. But I don't want to do it with Elbert watching us. We're not a movie."

"I understand. I'll walk you to the trailer and meet Elbert."

"Not tonight," I said. "Next time. I don't want to have to deal with Elbert. I've already embarrassed us both tonight, and I don't want Elbert to top it off."

He patted my hand, got out, went around and opened my door. I climbed out and smiled at him. I said, "Call me. Oh. Wait. My cell phone is dead. Or will be."

"They charge up, you know," he said.

"If you can afford to pay for the service they work fine."

"Oh," he said. "That's all right, then. I'll find you. I'll leave my number for you at the Dairy Bob. You can call me from there or something. I'll come by sometime."

"Okay," I said. "Goodnight, Herb."

"Goodnight, Dot."

I strolled away from him then, wishing I had kissed him in spite of Elbert. Behind me I heard his car pull out of the drive.

I stalked across the yard, heading quickly for the door, trying to only look at Elbert enough to be polite. As I came close to the chair where he was sitting, he said, "No kiss?"

"What?"

"You didn't kiss him. Date must have sucked."

"I thought you told me to take my time, or that he was a demon or something."

"Sit down, visit with me," Elbert said.

"I really ought to go in. I have to work tomorrow."

"Just for a minute. I'm lonely out here."

"Talk to Frank," I said.

"He's gone in for the night," Elbert said.

"Want me to wake him up for you?" I said.

"Earlier, he hit me with a water balloon," he said. "Just came out of the trailer and hit me with it, and then ran away."

"He does that," I said. "It's nothing personal."

I saw a curtain in the living room pull back. There was a little light in the trailer and it framed Mom in the window. I lifted a hand and waved. She waved back and pulled the curtain.

"They've been waiting for you to get back," Elbert said.

I wasn't surprised. They'd want to know about the date, and I didn't want to tell them all the details. I thought I'd just stall for awhile outside with Elbert.

"Come on, sit," Elbert said.

I sat. Elbert asked, "Was he okay?"

"He was okay." And then it started to come out. "Have you ever been on a date and acted like a psycho?"

I hadn't wanted to say that much, but I decided I'd rather talk to someone I didn't know well about it, than someone I did.

"I don't think so," he said. "I've been on some bad dates, but I don't think I acted like a psycho. A fool, maybe. But a psycho? Nope."

"Do you mention you're a bank robber on first dates?" I asked.

"Frankly, dear, I haven't had that many dates since I was a robber. And I doubt it's something I'd mention right away. I think it might be considered a conversation stopper."

"Yeah," I said. "I can see that. Third date? You'd mention it then?"

"Absolutely," he said, and grinned at me. "So, did you do something stupid?"

"I kind of flipped out. A little. Herb took hold of my hand, and I decided I'd have a litter of puppies and live in the back room of the trailer with Grandma for the rest of my life, so I jumped out of the car and yelled at him and tried to walk home. Then we had coffee and went bowling and came home. I think he's going to ask me out again."

"That's interesting," Elbert said. "Especially the part about a litter of puppies."

"That was symbolic," I said.

"Yeah," Elbert said. "I got that."

"Don't tell Mom or Grandma about it, will you?"

"Of course not," he said.

"And it goes without saying, don't tell Frank."

"I wouldn't tell Frank."

"Good, and that's all I want to say about the date."

"All right," he said.

I reached down and pulled up a weak brown piece of grass and twiddled it between my thumb and forefinger.

"Let me ask you something," I said. "You said you skated. But how good a skater are you?"

"I am so good I hurt figure skaters' feelings," he said.

"Really?"

"Not really. But I am good. I did tricks on the rink when I was a clown. I can skate with wheels, and I can skate with ice skates. I have good balance. My mother claimed it was because my head was empty."

"I skate pretty good, but what I want to learn is to skate like a roller derby skater."

"Did that." he said.

"What?" I said.

"Skated with a roller derby."

"Get out of town," I said. "You were a skating girl?"

"Guy, but yeah," he said. "I did that. Before I was a clown I was in a roller derby league."

"I thought it was just girls," I said.

"Seems to be these days, but wasn't always. I was part of the Houston Downtown Bombers."

"Were you a good team?"

Elbert shook his head. "No. Not really. I don't think we ever won anything. Sometimes we got paid to throw an event since it was mostly entertainment, but to the best of my memory, we never paid anyone else to throw one. So we didn't ever win anything. We kind of just quit. Our jammer, that's what they call the main skater, got a can of green beans thrown at him. Good toss. Hit him right upside the head. He was wearing a helmet, but it was still a good lick."

"Holy cow, people throw green beans?"

"Not as part of the sport, no. Someone who was for the other side brought the can to throw, and she had a good arm."

"She?" I said.

"Old lady. Former softball player."

"You're kidding, right?" I asked.

Elbert held up his hand. "No."

"Wait, you said you were paid to throw the game?"

"We were," he said.

"But why would you do that?" I asked.

"Money."

"You threw a game for money?"

"Honey, I'm a robber," Elbert said. "Well, attempted bank robber. Throwing a roller derby game for money does kind of fit in with my skill set. Anyway, our jammer that got hit with the can of beans, he quit, decided it was too risky. I got the clown job, and well, it was all over. The Houston Downtown Bombers were done with. We were actually from Cleveland, Texas anyway. Or at least a couple of the skaters were. I can't remember about the others. Me, I'm a rolling stone, so I wasn't really from anyplace specific. The team fell apart and we never won anything, but that doesn't mean I wasn't a good skater. We were just unfortunate and we sold out a lot. But why you want to do roller derby?"

"You said it," I said. "Money."

"You're throwing the match?"

"No. We're not throwing the match. We get money if we win," I said.

"What if you don't win?"

I shrugged. "Then we don't get any money."

Me and Elbert talked for a long while, and he tried to explain the rules of roller derby to me, which were few by the way. It mostly had to do with someone going around and around and being protected by the others on the team, and everyone on the other team trying to stop them. And there was this one person, the jammer, who had to get through and make a round or some such to gain a point. Some of it stuck with me, some of it slid off the side of my head like a greasy rag.

Elbert had some skates, and he went inside his van to get them. He came back with them, pushed them at me, said, "These are the best," he said.

"Not my brand," I said.

"No, your brand is a cheap brand, and I'm surprised you haven't turned your ankle."

"Unless you have another pair my size that's your brand," I said. "I'm kind of stuck with them."

"Where can we skate?" he asked. "I'll show you how it's done."

(22)

That's how we ended up going to the Dairy Bob. It was open, of course, and we went in and Bob was there. I wondered if he ever slept. Sometimes he would go away for a few hours and come back, so I guess he catnapped. He said something once about the war and how it had changed his sleeping. I didn't ask for details. I didn't get the idea he wanted to talk about it anyway.

Inside, Elbert bought me and him a hamburger. I had had a nice meal earlier, but now it was past midnight, and I had the munchies.

A short, stout, blonde girl named Miranda waited on us. She didn't have any outside traffic, and she had taken off her skates and had on tennis shoes. Sometimes, we did that, just to give our feet a rest. Bob only allowed so much of it, though. He had this whole thing about if you're on your feet then you're on the skates. Bob could skate okay himself. He was the one taught me how.

Miranda put our burgers and drinks down, looked at me, smiled, said, "We've met. You work here."

"Yeah," I said. "We've never had a shift together, but I've seen you around. This is my uncle, Elbert."

"Hey, Uncle Elbert," she said.

"Hey," he said back.

"I know Gay," Miranda said, "and she told me about the roller derby thing. I want you to know, you need me, I want in. My mom follows roller derby. We've gone to a few events, and she watches some stuff on the internet. My dad likes it too."

"So you know the game," I said.

"Yeah," she said. "Sorta."

"I never even heard of roller derby," I said, "and now it seems there's people all over that know about it."

"Roller girls," she said. "There's a kind of sisterhood of them. We'd be part of it. Gay might not be a big part of it. She's worried about her nose."

"I know," I said. "It is a nice nose."

"I just wanted to say I'm in," Miranda said. "I'll get you some ketchup for the fries."

We ate and went out back to the big parking lot. It was dead empty, except for my car and Miranda's and Bob's. There was a lot of concrete and it was all lit up by overhead lights on poles. There was a metal bar that separated the parking lot from the place where you could go through the drive-through.

Elbert sat on the separating bar and took off his shoes and put on his skates. I sat down beside him and started to put on mine.

"Wait before you do," he said. "I'll show you a few moves."

He went out on his skates and started skating. I could see right away he was smooth. He went left and right in a zig-zag pattern, said, "You'll need to do this for derby."

He got low and skated so that his arms swung out. He bobbed his head, like a snake trying to locate a mouse. He slammed a skate forward and spun, and went back in the other direction. It was all very quick and silky, like a dancer.

"I can do that on ice," he said.

"If we need that," I said. "We'll pull you up front."

He grinned at me. "I love to skate."

He darted around some more, and it was a pleasure to watch. When he moved, when he skated, I felt as if I was watching something unnatural become natural. As if he had been born with skates on his feet.

He said, "I can take some jumps too."

Elbert started at the far end of the lot and came toward me, and then he leaped. It was hard to see when he paused to do it. He just did it. He went up and forward, and hit on the skates and swiveled and was suddenly going in the other direction.

"I'll never learn to do that," I yelled after him.

When he came back my way, he said, "Probably not."

"Thanks for the faith," I said.

"Just that it takes time. A lot of it. You just want to win a derby match. The bar you're sitting on. I can jump it."

I looked down at the bar. It was about two foot high. "I believe you," I said.

"I'll show you."

He backed off again and came at it, and I realized he was coming right at me. I started to move, but held my ground, because I didn't really know what else to do.

He dodged around me and went to my left. It was a very speedy move. He leapt, and went over the bar, landed, sailed around on the concrete there, wheeled back my way, said, "I might go through the drive-through, order a soda."

I laughed at him. He jumped back over the bar. He skated around the parking lot still talking to me. He wasn't even breathing hard.

"You know what," he said. "I've always wanted to do a backwards jump. Never tried it. But I'm going to do it."

"I wouldn't," I said.

He wasn't listening. He came at me again, skating backwards, looking over his shoulder. I decided I would move this time.

Then he was right on the bar, and he leaped.

He went up high and he coiled his legs under him. His left skate was a little low. It caught the back of the bar and Elbert went backwards and hit the concrete hard. His head bounced.

"Oh, hell," he said.

After I went inside the Dairy Bob and got the phone and called, it took the ambulance about three minutes.

When we drove up in the yard, it was about four in the morning. I had work later in the afternoon, so it wasn't so bad for me. Elbert, on the other hand, had to have the back of his head shaved and there was a big bandage taped to it.

I stopped the car. Before I got out, Elbert said, "Don't tell your people, okay?"

"They're going to notice you have a bandage about the size of a bed sheet on the back of your head."

"I guess."

"No guessing about it, Elbert. They'll notice."

"I'll explain it to them. I think I'll tell them I fell down in the van."

"Why not just tell them the truth?" I asked.

"I'm not used to it," he said.

"Oh," I said. "Well, look at it this way, you were doing good there for awhile. A lot of smooth moves. I was impressed."

"Were you?" he asked.

"Oh yeah," I said.

"I really thought I could make that jump."

"I bet."

"I had never tried it backwards before, but I knew I could do it. Just knew it."

"Maybe next time you try it you could put a mat on the other side, or have some place where there's some soft dirt."

"Good idea."

"You know what surprises me most," I said.

"What?"

"You had insurance? We don't even have insurance. Can't afford it. I mean, something happens to me at the Dairy Bob, Bob has insurance, but I trip out here on the lawn... If you can call it a lawn, I'm on my own."

"When I had a job I paid up for a year," Elbert said. "A few months from now, I'm out of insurance. We'll be in the same club."

"You really skate well. You want to be our coach?"

"For the derby?"

"No. The annual spelling bee. Yes, the derby."

"Sure," he said. "I'd like that."

"But no backwards jumps over metal bars, okay?"

"Okay," he said. He picked up his skates, which he had laid on the seat, and got out of the car. As we were walking he laughed out loud.

"What is it," I said.

"Back at the emergency room," he said. "They gave me the wrong shoes. I didn't even notice till now. I'm wearing some other guy's shoes."

We both laughed then.

(24)

As I said, I didn't have work early the next morning, so I slept in. When I woke up I felt like my head was stuffed with cotton. I lay in bed for a moment and thought about the date the night before and the kiss I had missed. I was some piece of work. I lay there a long time before I got up and dressed. I got my clothes out of the closet, and when I pushed them back on the rack I could look at the derby poster. I had taped it up there, behind the clothes. I liked looking at it. I tried to imagine the girl on the poster as me. So far, hadn't been successful doing that, as she looked tough as a free steak, but I kept working on it.

In the kitchen Elbert, still wearing the patch on the back of his head, was at the table dipping a spoon into a bowl of cereal, talking with his mouth full. Mom had gone to work, and Frank was watching TV on the couch. He didn't even look at me when I came into the room. I'd be glad when summer was over and he was back in school.

Grandma was sitting at the table with Elbert, sitting in a chair that was sagging under her weight. She was laughing. She shook so much when she laughed I was afraid the chair was going to explode.

"You didn't say that?" she said.

"I did," he said. "I said just that."

Elbert lifted his eyes at me, and Grandma turned her head and said, "Elbert was just telling me how he hit his head."

"Were you?" I said to Elbert.

"He said he did it skating," Grandma said. "That he was trying to show you a jump at the Dairy Bob."

"That's right," I said. Elbert had told the truth. I was pleasantly surprised.

"He was telling me a funny thing he said to a nurse," Grandma said. "He has such a sense of humor."

I didn't remember anything funny he had said to a nurse, so maybe I was pleasantly surprised for a reason. I got a bowl and spoon and sat down at the table and poured milk and cereal.

"How was your date?" Grandma said. "Are you in love?"

"No, I'm not in love," I said. "But it was good. He was nice." I decided not to mention how odd I had acted, and hoped Elbert hadn't spilled the beans.

"Seeing him again?" she asked.

"Maybe," I said.

"Must not have been that good a date," Grandma said.

"You put me off boys, and now you want me to date one," I said.

"No," Grandma said. "I want you to finish school. You'd be the first of us to do it. Not a one in the family has ever got past the tenth grade, unless you count six months your mother had in the eleventh but had to drop out because she had you. Also, now that I think about it, she spent most of that six months in detention for one thing or another. That's where dating boys gets you."

"She wasn't dating boys when she was in detention," I said.

"Detention ended at three-thirty, Miss Smarty Pants," Grandma said.

"Not everyone who dates gets pregnant." I said.

"No," Grandma said. "But it seems in this family they do."

"Maybe we need to change our water supply," I said. "It could be in the water."

"Trust me," Grandma said, "it isn't."

I decided there was nowhere to go with the conversation, so I said to Elbert, "So, you going to teach me some of those skating moves from last night, minus the part where you try and jump a rail and smack your head and go to the hospital?"

"Absolutely," he said.

"Sure you're up to it?" I asked.

"I skate with my feet, not my head."

"Last night you didn't," I said.

"Yeah, well, there was a moment there," Elbert said.

We ate and drove over to an abandoned lot where cars had once been sold. A few years back the car lot had gone out of business, and so far no one else had taken over. There were some newspapers and soda cups being pushed around in the lot by the wind.

We put on our skates, and Elbert began to give me pointers. He showed me how to swirl around him when he came up alongside me. How to cut him off with sharp angles. He showed me how to turn real quick and skate backwards. Showboating, he called it. He said you got ahead and you wanted to give the spectators a little something cool to look at, and thumb your nose at the other team, that's what it was for. He said, truth was, it was risky and probably ought to be avoided and he wished he hadn't shown it to me. I learned how to do it anyway.

He showed me all manner of tricks. I did pretty well the first day, and by week's end I was styling a little. I talked to the other girls, and got in contact with Miranda, and we started having Elbert train us. We weren't always able to work as a team, but as many of us as could manage to get together at one time did.

When Gay first got there, she had on some cute shorts and a kind of dressy top, like maybe she was going to a photo shoot for sportswear. Elbert had used his own money, wherever that came from, and bought us all knee pads and he had us put them on.

We were going to get helmets next. Right now the rule was don't fall on our heads.

When Gay had on her knee pads, she said, "Don't I get a stick?"

"That's hockey," I said.

"Oh," Gay said.

"And they skate on ice," I said. "We don't."

"Oh, okay," Gay said.

Gay was terrible. She could skate all right, but she didn't have any idea of the rules, no matter how many times Elbert explained them to her. Elbert had used chalk to draw a kind of roller rink on the concrete. It wasn't what we needed, of course, but it was something. Gay kept thinking you could skate either way, and she couldn't understand the concept of the chalk lines as the roller rink. When anyone got close to her, even if they weren't touching her, she laughed like she was being tickled.

"Maybe we can use her as back up," Elbert said. "You know, in case all the rest of you die, or something."

We practiced pretty hard. I was doing better than anyone else in the skating department, and started to get a bit cocky. Herb came out to watch a few times, and of course that made me show off a little.

We girls started working together well enough, though, as I said, we didn't always have all of us in the same place at once. That was the next part of our plan, to have more than three at a time show up. As Elbert explained, it took five to make a team, not three.

Raylynn turned out to be a fierce competitor. Or would have been, had we had a team to play against. Right now we were just working drills to understand better how to skate. Still, sometimes I skated alongside of her, and we did this drill where she tried to get past me, and she always did. She usually managed to do it in such a way that I got a bruise or two and we exchanged curse words as we went around in a circle.

"A lot of anger in you two," Elbert said about me and sis.

Raylynn said, "You know, this makes me feel good. When I'm out there, I feel pretty much in control. Like I could skate around the world, and only stop once for a light lunch."

"That's good," Elbert said.

"I think so," Raylynn said. "Yeah. I think so."

(25)

Later that week I had some of the cockiness knocked out of me at work. I was skating up to a car, and a guy sitting on the driver's side, not looking, opened the door right in front of me. I guess he was going to get out and use the restroom or something. But the thing is, he was talking to the guy sitting on the passenger side, and didn't see me, and suddenly, there was the door.

I had a tray full of food. I lifted it high with one hand, and shifted on my skates. Let me tell you, it was a thing of beauty. I went right around that door, using a move Elbert had taught me. I thought, wow, cool, because I was as graceful as that Greek god with the winged shoes. My body swayed perfectly. I balanced the tray without losing the drink on it, or a single French fry. I was grace in motion.

Then a lady in another car on my right side, opened her passenger door. I caught it full square. The tray went flying and so did I. As the old joke goes, the ground broke my fall. I somehow twisted my ankle in the skate. The pain was so intense I passed out. The last thing I remember right before I blacked out was a full cup of ice and soda, a fist full of French fries falling down on me; in that hazy moment the ice cubes looked like large diamonds and the fries like thin fingers.

When I came awake Bob was bending over me, brushing off ice and French fries. "Dot? You okay? Dot?"

"Not so much," I said.

"You hit a door."

"I kind of figured that," I said.

"You dropped a tray of food," he said.

"Pity," I said.

I tried to get up with Bob's help, but no luck. My ankle was twisted and it burned like fire. I had concrete raspberries on my elbows and one of my knees; I could feel the rawness of it rubbing up against the inside of my jeans. I felt like I was going to throw up.

Bob picked me up like a baby and carried me into the Dairy Bob and sat me in a booth with my foot sticking out. He went in the back and got a mop bucket and turned it over and raised my foot up on it.

In the moment he had carried me, I remembered times when I fell asleep on the couch, watching television, and my dad had picked me up carefully and toted me to bed and tucked me in, patted my head before he went out. I never opened my eyes during all that time, because I didn't want him to make me walk and miss out on being in his arms, I felt safe. I thought it would always be like that.

It was an odd feeling, and I felt like crying, and did a little. Bob thought it was because of the pain in my foot.

"Wait here," Bob said, as if I had a lot of choice.

Bob went outside. The two cars, the one with the man, and the other with the woman, had driven off. They didn't even leave a note. Maybe some gas fumes, but no note.

When Bob came back inside, he said, "You okay?"

"Of course I'm not okay," I said. "I'm the same injured girl I was two minutes ago."

"Your mouth still works," he said.

I was unlacing my skates. The skate on the uninjured foot came off easy, but the other didn't. It had already swollen too much. Trying to pull it off hurt like fire.

Bob went in back, came out with a pair of scissors large enough to trim trees, and went to work on the skate. "I can't afford new ones, Bob."

"I can." He cut the skate off and gently examined my foot. It looked like a full grown turkey stuffed tight in a sock.

"That's not good," he said. "It makes me a little sick to look at it."

"Don't hold back, Bob," I said. "Don't spare my feelings."

"I wasn't," he said, not understanding that I was being sarcastic. Bottom line was it hurt, and it hurt bad and I was a little scared it was broken.

Bob left Sue in charge and drove me to the hospital, right where Elbert and I had been a few nights back. They X-rayed me and looked me over and said I had a bad sprain, but no break. They gave me a kind of reinforced shoe to wear. It was big and had a lot of foam it. It had metal braces on the sides.

The doctor who came in and looked at me and told me not to skate for a few weeks. I thought: Really, did he think I was going to strap on some skates right then and go for it?

When it came time to pay, they put me in a wheelchair and wheeled me to the reception desk. Bob showed them his insurance card. It was the first time in my life there had ever been insurance for anything. I thought if I had had the injury in that old car lot, they'd have had to put me down like a broken-legged horse in those old Western movies.

Anyway, I got to go home. I guess that was all right, but the bad part was I wasn't making any money. If I wasn't making any money, then the whole family lost out. And I couldn't skate. I couldn't get ready for the derby.

When I finally pulled the doctor's shoe off, pulled on my pajamas and got in bed with my foot wrapped, I felt pretty blue. Elbert, with a fresh patch on the back of his head, sat in a chair beside the bed and talked to me for awhile, told me how I shouldn't worry about the roller derby thing, there would be other times, and so on. That just made me feel worse. I didn't want other times. I wanted the time coming up.

"I'm not giving up yet," I said.

"I didn't think you would," Elbert said. "You don't seem much like a quitter, but I thought a pep talk was in order."

"Sometimes I feel cursed," I said. "No matter what plan I have it goes awry."

"Welcome to life," Elbert said. "Thing I learned is we all focus on the things that go wrong and not on the things that go right."

"Coming from a bank robber," I said, "that's very inspiring."

"It was an attempted robbery," he said.

"Yeah, okay. That's right."

"On that note, kid," Elbert said. "I'm going to leave you be. I have to go sit in the yard."

Grandma made me some dinner, and it was awful, as all her dinners are. I thanked her and ate it anyway.

Raylynn was about to leave for her shift at the Dairy Bob, which had been moved to an earlier time because I was out of business. When Bob brought me home he didn't hesitate to ask her to come into work a little early.

She stopped in to see me before she left. I said, "Sorry, Raylynn. You work plenty. Sorry."

"I can use the money," she said, taking the chair where Elbert had sat. "We all could. And, I have a little apartment I'm going to rent."

"Really?" I said.

"Yeah. It's small, and it's a second story thing. I have to climb stairs everyday, tote the baby up, but I'm moving in next week. I put down a little deposit. They're supposed to get rid of the smell."

"The smell?" I said.

"Dead raccoon or something," she said. "In the attic. There's a hole in the roof, too. That's how the raccoon got in. He gnawed through some wires and was barbecued."

"Poor thing," I said.

"Yeah, well, they got to repair the hole in the roof, but you know, it's all right. I like it. I will like it. There's enough room for me and the kids if one of us sleeps under the kitchen table."

I laughed. It was enough to shake me and make my foot hurt.

Frank came in then. "Can I sign your cast?" he said.

"I don't have a cast," I said. "I have a shoe."

"Let me sign the shoe," he said.

"No, I don't want the shoe signed."

"I could be the first," he said.

"No," I said. "I'm not going to have the shoe signed."

"I want to be first, not second," he said.

"If no one signs it you won't be first, second or third," I said.

"Come on, let me," he said.

"Would you go on, you little fart," Raylynn said.

"Witch," Frank said.

"Weasel," Raylynn said.

Frank started to say something else, but Raylynn jumped up and moved like she was going to go after him. He darted out of the room.

Raylynn grinned at me. "He still remembers when I used to chase him down and tickle him. He hates that. Look. I got to go. But, well, I don't have much gas in my car. I'm down to fumes. Can I borrow yours?"

"Sure," I said. "See you later," and away she went.

Grandma brought me some magazines. They were about as interesting as dyeing a mouse's hair. I dozed off and on.

Later in the day there was a knock on my bedroom door. I said, "Come in," thinking it would be Mom home from work, but it was Herb.

I hate to admit it, but I was mortified. There I was in my pajamas with little dogs designs on them, in a little bed with old sheets and blankets, in a room in a trailer, and there was Herb who ate at fine restaurants and traveled all over the world and felt good about himself and was so nice-looking it made my back teeth ache, and he was staring at me.

"Hi," I said. I know. It's nothing special, but that's all I had in me right then.

Herb came and sat in the chair by the bed.

"You didn't have to come by," I said.

"I know that," he said.

"You found out awful quick," I said.

"I heard about it from Bob."

"How?" I asked.

"He was coming into the Dairy Bob, and I was already there. I was looking for you, and the girl working there...Sue?"

"Yeah," I said. "Sue."

"She said you went to the hospital. I sort of panicked and was heading over there, but before I left, in came Bob. He told me you were home, and so I came over. How'd it happen?"

"I was dancing nude in the highway and got hit by a truck."

Herb laughed a little. More than the comment deserved, but I was glad he did.

"I hate I missed that," he said. "The nude part. Not getting hit by a truck."

Then I told him how it really happened.

We talked for awhile, about this and that. It wasn't long before I felt a lot less self-conscious about where I was, about the way things looked. Herb had a kind of calming factor about him. I needed that. I was always revved up and a little angry about something or another, just like Elbert had said about me and Raylynn.

After a bit, the door opened, and Mama came in. "Oh, baby, are you all right?"

So we went through it all again, me explaining what happened, introducing her to Herb.

Herb stood up from his chair and touched my shoulder and said, "I got to go. I have to study for a test. I'm doing a summer class. I'll check back."

"Thanks, Herb," I said, and he went out and closed the door.

Mom said, "Oh, boy. He's a good-looking one."

"Yep, his looks don't hurt my feelings at all," I said. "And he seems like a nice guy. Are there such things as nice guys, Mama?"

"I've heard tell of them," Mama said. "They say, they exist in the deep woods, and are rarer than fairies and unicorns."

"How do you think Frank is going to turn out?" I said.

Mama wagged her hand a little, like a boat on the ocean.

"It could go either way," she said.

No wonder I'm such a pessimist.

(26)

The days went by slow and tedious, like dragging a dead cow up a hill with a thin rope. I read some books, and was able to limp onto the couch and watch some television, but there really wasn't anything I wanted to see. Frank usually owned the set anyway so he could play his video games. He had four of them and he had played them so much I doubt there was any real challenge. Still, he clicked away in front of the couch, jumping up now and then to sort of dance around as he worked the controls. He liked to yip like a coyote too. There's no explaining boys.

Raylynn had moved with the kids to her new apartment. That gave a lot more room in the trailer, but it also seemed more empty, lonely.

It was easier to spend time in bed feeling sorry for myself.

By the way, the shoe for my sprain had been signed by Frank without my knowing it. I hurt too bad to give him grief.

One thing I did do was I took my laptop to bed, got it connected to the internet and looked up some things just for fun. I read about fish that could walk on land and a spider that poisoned wasps in such a way the spider could lead the wasp by one antenna like a zombie. The spider would walk it to its lair, so to speak, and feed it to its young.

Told you I was bored.

Every afternoon I took a walk, using crutches that Mama got me from the Goodwill, and Elbert would walk with me. We just walked through the trailer park. I couldn't go far. Elbert carried a switch in case any dogs wanted to bite us. I think they all did. I guess dogs hate seeing a young girl on two sticks. The patch on the back of his head had gotten smaller as the days passed, and now it was gone.

"What kind of guy was my dad?" I asked him.

"Oh, I don't know. He was all right I guess. You remember him. You weren't a baby when he left."

"I didn't take a lot of notes about him, though. I wasn't expecting him to run like a deer."

"He was all right," Elbert said again.

"Can you throw me a bone here?" I said.

"Okay. He talked about you and your sister."

"What did he say?"

"That he loved you."

"If he loved us so much, why did he run off?"

Elbert shook his head. "I can't explain that. There should be some easy answer, I guess, but I don't know what it is."

"Did you ask him whey he ran off?"

"Not really," Elbert said. "Not directly. I guess I didn't know how to ask."

"You open your mouth and you say, 'Hey, why did you run off from your girls you claim to love so much?'"

"Yeah, well," Elbert said, "it's a lot easier talking about it here than it was then. Maybe he thought you'd be better off without him."

"Oh, wow," I said. "That's like the boy who breaks up with you and says it's not you, it's him. He has to find himself. But what he really means is he has to chase after some blonde, but he doesn't want to say that."

"Is that your experience?"

"No," I said. "That's really Raylynn's experience, but since we're sisters, I think it's an experience close enough to borrow.

Let me ask you. Was there another woman? Is that why dad left? Was he cheating on Mom?"

"Wish I had some answers," Elbert said, shrugging. "But I don't."

"Was he nice otherwise?" I asked.

"Nice? Yeah. I guess. I mean, he was nice enough. Me and him got along okay."

"That doesn't sound like a lot of brotherly love going on there," I said.

Elbert looked at the ground. "We weren't that close. Not really...Dot, I know this isn't what you want to hear, but you should let it go. The man made a choice. A bad choice. But it's done. There are some things you can't fix, can't go back on. A choice like that, it's one of them."

"It would be nice to know what it was we did wrong," I said.

I paused to reposition my crutches. My underarms were getting chaffed. We started out again.

"Here's the thing, and this I'm certain of, girl," Elbert said. "You didn't do anything wrong. None of you did. Frankly, your dad loved you, but not enough. And that was his fault. Not yours. He's a low-life bastard and that's all there is to it. Same as Raylynn's boyfriend. What's that dip's name?"

"Tim," I said.

"Same as him. That's how he is. Maybe he didn't hit your mother...I don't know. Didn't hit you... Again, I don't know."

"He didn't," I said.

"All right," Elbert said. "He had that going for him. But he didn't have any character. He didn't know how to do the right thing because he's one of those that doesn't know the right thing exists. Not really."

"Is it how you two were raised?" I said.

Elbert stopped walking. He turned and looked at me as I stopped and leaned on my crutches. "You know what I think?" he said. "I think we're all responsible for what we do. It isn't someone else's fault. It isn't always genetics or how our parents' treated you, because there's plenty born to bad circumstances with all manner of things wrong with them, and they don't all turn out to be crumbs. We choose to be who we are. We make ourselves into who we want to be."

"Are you who you want to be?"

"Not by a long shot," Elbert said.

(27)

I don't know exactly why I hadn't thought of it before, but now with nothing but boredom to fill my days, it occurred to me that I might make a search for my dad. It was either that or sit with Grandma in the living room and watch game shows and smell her gas, or play video games with Frank, the Booger Eater.

The search had no real expectation on my part, but I thought it would be something to do; as always, it was on my mind. It was just that now I had slowed down long enough to give it some true consideration. I thought, what if I use one of those search engines that locates people on the internet?

The idea bounced around in my head, and finally I got the one credit card I have, one that holds about two hundred dollars, and propped myself up in bed with my old laptop. The card was one of those they like to offer high school students so they can get them hooked on using credit cards and going into deep debt. Or that was what Mama said. She said, first it's two hundred dollars, but if you use it and you pay it off, then your credit score rises, and the next thing you know you've booked a trip to Berlin and bought a Siberian Husky, a parakeet and clothes you'll never wear, and you owe the credit card company a zillion dollars, not counting the interest.

I considered all of that, and decided I was only going to use it to get on one of the search sites, and then pay it all off when the bill came in. I didn't think it could cost that much, and by then I would have some money stored away.

Considering how little money I made, this was a chancy enterprise. Still, I wanted to know what had happened to Dad. I figured the bottom line was I'd owe a bill and find out absolutely nothing for my troubles.

I used the card, got logged in, typed in his name, and immediately it came up. Now, our last name isn't all that odd, but my dad's first name, Jethro is a little more unlikely. But still, it's not that someone else couldn't be named that. This man with the same name lived in Bullard. That was near Tyler. I had been through Bullard, or at least its outskirts, just the other day when I went shopping in Tyler.

I held my breath.

Could it be?

Surely not.

Nothing could be that simple. He went out for a pack of cigarettes and ended up in Bullard, Texas? Not far from where we lived right now?

It had to be a different Jethro Sherman.

If it was him, the idea that he had only gone a few miles away from us somehow hit me harder than if he had moved to Alaska to study polar bears.

I looked to see how many Jethro Shermans popped up. There were only two, and one was listed as being seventy-three. That wouldn't be him unless he had gotten caught in a time warp, lived somewhere else for years, and came back to our time and decided to live in Bullard. But that Jethro was listed as living in Little Rock, Arkansas, not Bullard, so time travel was most likely out. The man in Bullard was exactly the right age to be Dad. He was listed as a Handy Man. Dad had been good at fixing things, when he wanted to do it, which wasn't that often. He hadn't had a job the day he went out for cigarettes, just a nicotine habit.

I looked at the address some more and thought about how easily I could drive over there and find him. I thought about what I would say to him if it was in fact Dad. I figured the real truth was it would be a different man.

I sat there and thought about a lot of things, and finally I dozed, and when I awoke, it was to Grandma moving around in the room.

"You might want to get up and crutch into the kitchen," Grandma said. "Alma's home and she's fixing dinner."

"Can she bring it here?" I said.

"She could," Grandma said, "but she told me you'd ask, and she told me to tell you no."

"I have an injured foot," I said.

"Yes, and it'll get well faster if you don't nurse it all the time."

"It's not like I'm going to walk on it," I said. "I'll use crutches. Why can't I just stay in bed?"

"Because you sound depressed and you don't need to be depressed," she said, "your mother and I do enough of that for the entire family."

The lap top was still resting on my lap, so I put it aside, and was about to get out of bed when Mama came into the room with a tray. Grandma looked at her like a mongoose looks at a cobra.

"I thought you said she had to get up," Grandma said.

"I did," Mama said. "But I changed my mind. I feel like spoiling her a little."

"And I feel like being spoiled," I said.

"Well," Grandma said, "I'll leave the two of you to the spoiling. I'm going to join Elbert and Frank at the table."

"I'll be there in a moment," Mama said.

"Suit yourself," Grandma said, and went out of the room.

I positioned myself up in bed, and Mama put the tray where the lap top had been. It was pinto beans and cornbread, a side of creamed corn. My favorite.

"Thanks, Mama," I said.

"Fixed it just for you," she said. "Are you doing all right?"

"Just bored. Mama, when Daddy left, did you look for him?"

Mama sat down in the chair by the bed. She said, "Not much. I figured he wanted to be here he would. That doesn't mean I didn't miss him, but it meant I didn't think I ought to chase him down."

"Are you going to divorce him?"

"I think about it. But you know…and I don't like this about myself…I keep thinking he'll come back. And worse, I keep thinking I'll be glad to see him."

"Do you think something happened to him?" I asked.

Mama shook her head. "No. I think he left because he wanted to leave. I think he's out there."

"And you still want him to come back?" I asked.

"It's foolish, but I do. The heart is a really complicated and not too smart instrument."

"It's actually the brain that decides these things," I said. "Not the heart."

"Yeah, well, I like to think it is actually the heart," Mama said, "because I prefer to believe my brain isn't so stupid as to put up with the idea of him coming back. How do you feel about it?"

"I miss him. And I'm mad at him. I'm mostly confused."

"Sometimes life isn't fair, baby girl," she said.

She stood up from the chair. "Should I shut the door?"

I could hear the TV blaring in the other room. "Sure, shut it. That would be fine."

When she was gone I ate my food, moved the tray and put the laptop on my lap again and looked up my father's name one more time, looked at the address in Bullard.

Later I crutched outside and found Elbert sitting in his chair, nursing a can of beer. I pulled up the other lawn chair, said, "You used to be a detective. Can you find your brother? My daddy?"

"I wasn't a very good detective," he said.

"Well, let me put it this way, I've already found him."

"Then why would you ask me?"

"Because I don't really need someone to find him, but it seemed like a conversation starter."

"What do you need?" Elbert asked.

"Company."

"You're sure it's him, Dot?"

"I think I've found him. I have the name and the address, and it isn't far from here."

"Perhaps you should leave well enough alone," Elbert said.

"He's your brother," I said. "Don't you want to see him?"

"No. As I said, we're not that close."

"All right, then," I said. "That's okay. But me, I'm going anyway."

I got up and started crutching toward the car.

"You're going now?" he said.

"No time like the present," I said.

When I got to the car, I heard him coming up behind me. "You shouldn't be driving with that foot," he said.

"Maybe so," I said. "But I'm going anyway."

"Dang it," Elbert said. "Get in. I'll drive."

(28)

We had barely reached the edge of Marvel Creek when a black cloud came rolling over our heads and started dropping rain and spitting lighting, coughing thunder.

"Another day might be better," Elbert said.

"I can take you home," I said. "But I'm going if I have to push the gas and the brake pedal with my crutch."

"You'd do it too, wouldn't you?"

"Yes."

"You are the most stubborn person I have ever met," he said.

We drove on, but the rain got really bad, and we had to pull over to the side of the road for awhile. We sat there with the motor running and the windshield wipers swatting, but not really managing much against the rain. The windshield was a sheet of water.

"You find him," Elbert said. "If it is him, things might not be how you want them."

"They're not how I want them now," I said. "Could they be worse?"

"They could," he said.

"You seem pretty determined to talk me out of finding him."

"I'm just trying to prepare you, Dot."

"I want answers," I said.

"There isn't an answer to everything," Elbert said. "Sometimes there's just a bigger mystery."

I let that thought whirl around in my head, but didn't have a response. I sat there and tried to remember all the good things about my dad. I hated to admit it, but it was a short list. I didn't really recall all that much at all. I remembered how he looked and that he had a good smile. I remembered how he had carried me to bed. I remembered him watching *The Wizard of Oz* on TV with me. I remembered him at the table eating. Mostly I remembered him going out and coming in. I remember always feeling like I was waiting for him. Then there was the time he went out and didn't come back.

We sat there until the rain slowed. I rolled down my window and felt the cool wind on my face, the smell of wet dirt. We were parked near a little culvert that ran under the highway, and water was running out of one end of it over some rocks; it made a sound like someone doodling around on a piano. Leaves washed along. One of them had a green and blue beetle riding on it, like a boat. After awhile the water quit running so fast. The leaves began to bunch up in the culvert. The beetle took that moment to make his escape onto the solid earth.

"I think we can go now," I said.

Elbert started back out on the highway, still letting the wipers slap at the rain, otherwise cruising in silence. I sneaked a glance at him from time to time. His forehead was wrinkled and his head was bent forward, as if he were about to close his eyes and push through a mess of cobwebs.

When we got to Bullard we stopped at a gas station and I got out on my crutches to pump gas in. Elbert took the nozzle from me and put it in himself. When he finished, he took out his wallet and started in to pay.

"I don't want you to pay," I said.

"I want to," he said. "And I don't want an argument."

"All right," I said. He gave me a look like a man standing on the deck of a sinking ship with his feet in leg irons, then went inside. I crutched in after him.

I asked the guy for directions to the street I wanted. I got back in the car and told Elbert how to get there, and away we went.

As we rode along, Elbert said suddenly. "You and me are friends, right?"

"Right," I said.

"I mean, friends sometimes see things different ways, right?"

"I suppose," I said. "What are you talking about, Elbert?"

"Nothing," he said.

The street wasn't really in Bullard. It was back and beyond the little town, and it was a dirt street with a bit of asphalt that had mostly washed away and left holes big enough to lose a volley ball in. There were trees along the streets, and they looked tired and sweaty from the rain. Already the sun was out, and it was hot, and things were drying fast. Heat mist came up from the earth.

Finally we came to the house. We drove past it and down the street, and back in front of it. We stopped across the street and took a look.

It wasn't a nice house. It was white but needed fresh paint. There was a red tricycle in the yard, or it had been red once. Now it was mostly rust-colored. There was a carport and an old Ford in the carport. The grass in the yard was grown up and damp with rain. One of the windows by the front door was taped over where it had been cracked. The roof was peeling, as if it had been sunburned bad and now the skin was coming off. There were birds in the yard, a bunch of them, pecking in the grass for insects and worms.

"Now you've seen it," Elbert said.

"I've seen the house," I said. "I haven't seen him."

"So, do you get out and knock on the door?"

"Maybe."

I sat there and thought about that, but wasn't quite up for it. Not yet.

"You hungry?" I said.

"Hungry?"

"Yeah. Let's eat first and come back. I'll work up my courage."

Elbert let out his breath, like someone fresh rescued from a deep dark pit. "All right," he said. "Let's do that."

But right then a man came out of the house, through the carport. He was pushing a lawn mower. He was a tall man, a nice-looking man, and though he seemed to have aged some, I knew who he was right away. It was my daddy.

addy pushed the mower out to the edge of the street and pulled the cord and started it up. He looked in our direction, but didn't take much notice. He started pushing the mower into the grass.

"That's dumb," Elbert said. "It's too wet to mow. All the grass will bunch up on the blade."

"What are you?" I said. "Ground maintenance?"

"Just an observation," he said.

I watched Daddy struggle with the mower, pushing it along. Elbert was right. It was too wet to mow.

"I'm going over," I said.

Elbert reached out and touched my arm. "You've seen him," he said. "You know where he is, that he's okay. You could just let it go."

"No," I said. "No, I can't."

I got out of the car on my crutches, worked my way across the street. I made it all the way to the edge of the property where Daddy was mowing. He had his back to me. He hadn't seen me come up, and he couldn't hear me because of the mower. I leaned there on my crutches.

I heard a car door slam behind me, and knew Elbert was coming over. His shadow fell down beside me.

It was uncomfortable just standing there, but I couldn't bring myself to go over and touch him, make him aware I was there. I waited until he turned the mower and saw me.

He did a kind of startle, like something had flown into his face. Then he stopped pushing the mower and stood there with his mouth open. He looked at me, then Elbert.

Finally, he swallowed. It was a big swallow. He hit a switch on the mower and turned it off. When he did, he didn't move. He just stood there, his hands on the mower handle.

"Hello," I said.

"Hello, Dot," he said. "You've grown."

"Yeah," I said. "It happened while you were gone. What are you doing here?"

He came across the yard then. He said, "I live here."

"I didn't think you had a job mowing the grass," I said. "We saw you come out of the house."

Daddy looked at Elbert. He said, "I don't get it. What are you doing here, Elbert?"

Elbert didn't answer. He just looked at the ground.

"Did you find your cigarettes?" I asked.

"I'm sorry, Dot," Daddy said.

"Why?" I said.

"Why what?" he said.

"Why what?" I said. "Did you actually say 'Why what'? You go out for cigarettes and disappear for years and I find you mowing a lawn in Bullard, and you say, 'Why what'?"

"How...how did you find me?" he asked.

"The internet," I said. "I found your name and address on the internet."

"Oh," he said.

"You don't want to see me?" I said.

"I didn't say that," he said.

"So, you been in Bullard, and you forgot where Marvel Creek was, or that you had a wife and daughter, and step daughter, and a son."

"How is your mother?"

"Waiting on you," I said.

"What happened to your foot?" Daddy asked.

"I fell down," I said. "Look, I didn't come here to talk about my foot."

Daddy looked at Elbert again. "I just don't understand why you're here, Elbert."

"There's some explaining to do," Elbert said. "It's complex."

"I'd rather not talk here," Daddy said. "Can we go into town. I can meet you there. Say, the Dairy Queen."

"Are you going to go there by way of around the world?" I asked. "Is this another one of those I'll be right back situations?"

He shook his head. "No. I live here. So, I'll come back." Somehow, him saying that hit me as hard as if I had been shot with an arrow through the heart. He had lived with us too, but that hadn't stopped him from going away.

"Please," he said. "I don't want to disturb anyone in the house."

"Disturb them?" I said, and I found myself lifting my crutch like I might hit Daddy with it. I had the same kind of anger going through me I had when I hit Tim with that two-by-four.

"It's all right," Elbert said, touching my shoulder. "We'll meet you there."

"No," I said. "It's not all right."

Daddy gave me a look that was as sad as any I had ever seen. I felt sorry for him in spite of myself.

"Oh, okay," I said. "But you better not run out on me, mister. You better not."

"I'll be there," he said.

We had passed the Dairy Queen when we were looking for Daddy's address, so we knew right where it was. When we got there we stayed in the car. About ten minutes after we arrived, Daddy pulled up in the old Ford. He got out and opened the back door of my car and slid in on the back seat, moving my crutches so he could.

"It's good to see you, Dot," he said.

"Is it?" I said.

He studied on my remark, said, "This is all so confusing."

"That's an understatement," I said. "Think how confusing it's been for me. I didn't know where you were. I don't know why you left. I thought maybe you were dead. Sometimes I hoped you were dead. And here you are, saying things are confusing, like you aren't the one made them that way."

"I did, didn't I?" he said. "I just don't understand why you're here with Elbert."

"Forget Elbert," I said. "You tell me, right now, why you left, and why you didn't come back."

"It won't be a very satisfying," he said.

"Told you," Elbert said.

"Tell me anyway."

"All right," he said, and leaned back against the seat. "I was unhappy."

I waited, but he didn't follow up.

"That's it?" I said. "You were unhappy. Had a bad day and just took off? Really? That's it?"

"Kind of."

"Come on, Daddy, you have to give me more than that."

I was turned with my arm over the seat, looking at him. He was leaned back tight against the backseat. He looked very small. Not like the big man I remembered.

"It wasn't you, and it wasn't Frank, and it wasn't Raylynn, or your mother," he said. "It was me."

"Of course it was you," I said. "But why was it you? What did we do?"

"Nothing," he said. "You didn't do a thing. I guess I just didn't feel I was where I wanted to be. I had nothing but junk jobs, and two kids to feed, a wife who was doing most of the work, and I felt bad about that. One morning, I had had enough, so I got up and left."

"But Mom didn't leave," I said. "What if she left? You don't think she isn't tired? That it isn't tough raising kids? You don't think that?"

"I know what I did," he said, "and I'm not proud of it."

"I certainly hope not," I said.

"Yeah," Elbert said, "that's cold."

"Elbert," I said. "You stay out of it."

"I still don't understand what he's doing here," Daddy said.

"So you left," I said. "Tell me the rest."

"I went to get cigarettes," he said. "That was my plan. But when I got to the store and bought a pack and was going to turn around and go home, I didn't. I just started driving. I had a bit of gas money, and I drove until I was in Arkansas. I didn't choose it, I just ended up there. Can I smoke?"

"No," I said, "you can not. Not in my car. Just finish your story."

"So I was in Arkansas and out of gas, and I had to leave the car where it was, a motel parking lot. I didn't even have money for my room, but they were looking for someone to clean rooms, so I started doing that. I guess I was there about six months, and then they fired me for something or another. I don't remember what, and I was on the road again. I guess I drove all over the South, and then I started back home."

"But you didn't make it?" I said.

"No. I didn't make it. I came across Elbert here."

"Came across," I said. "What does that mean?"

"I mean I met him in jail."

"You mean prison, right?" I said.

"No," Dad said. "Jail."

"I'm even more confused now," I said.

I looked at Elbert. He did a thing with his mouth that looked like he was trying to stick his bottom lip in behind his teeth so the rest of him could crawl in behind it. I turned back to Dad.

"I got picked up for vagrancy," he said. "That old car finally wore out and I sold it for junk, and then I was on foot. I hitch-hiked. People don't pick up hitchhikers that often, so it took me a long time to get back to Texas. But when I did get back, I didn't stop in East Texas. I kept going. I ended up in San Antonio, and that's where I got picked up for not having any visible means of support. I had about two dollars in my pocket, so I was glad to go to jail. And that's where I met Elbert."

"What are the odds?" I said.

"Odds?" Dad said.

"Of meeting your brother in jail like that," I said.

"Brother? He's not my brother."

I snapped a look at Elbert. "This is true, Dot. I may have lied a little bit."

"A little bit," I said. "You...you're not my uncle."

Elbert shook his head. "Nope, but I want to be."

My head was swimming. "I don't get it."

"Neither do I," Dad said.

"I didn't know him," Elbert said, "but there is a true coincidence here."

"Thank goodness for that," I said. I wanted to be mad, but I was too stunned.

"I actually do have the same last name," Elbert said. "So, we could be kin. Cousins or something."

"It's a common name," Dad said. "So, there we were in jail together, and when they let us out in a few days, told us to leave. We left together and decided we needed money, and so we tried to rob a beauty parlor."

"I thought it was a bank," I said.

"I may have exaggerated," Elbert said.

"We didn't have gun," Dad said, "and Elbert didn't have the heart to do it right, so this woman ran him out of there with a hair dryer."

"Not one of the big ones the women put their head under," Elbert said, just in case I might be suffering confusion, "but a small one, for close work."

"I was supposed to be a look out," Dad said, "but instead, while I'm looking, Elbert here nearly runs over me running from the lady with the hair dryer. So there we were, two grown men jogging down the street with a little woman chasing us with a hair dryer."

"She actually hit me a time or two," Elbert said. "Those things can hurt."

"Anyway, we got picked up again, and this time we went to jail and it looked like we'd go to prison, but since there was no gun, and we didn't get any money, and the judge sort of felt we were just stupid, not dangerous, we just spent some time in jail."

"Not prison?" I said.

"There's not a lot of difference," Elbert said.

"Oh, yes there is," I said.

"Anyway, when they let us out, I started back home, and I made it to Bullard. I got a job at a filling station there. I thought I'd come home with a little money in my pocket, and then I met Bonnie, and well, we been together ever since."

"Bonnie?" I said.

"We live together," Dad said.

"The tricycle in the yard," I said. "That your child's."

"Not by birth, no," Dad said. "But Bonnie had a little girl when we met. Her husband had run off."

"Like you," I said.

"Yes," Dad said. "Like me. And what I saw was a chance to start over, to fix things. To be a husband and a father. And I have been. I don't have much of a job, night shift at a store/filling station, some handy man work, but its honest work, and we get by. Here's something special, considering me and Elbert got chased by a lady with a hair dryer from a beauty shop. Bonnie is a beautician."

"Of course she is," I said. "So you took up with a woman with a child, and left your wife and two children, and just started over, doing not so much that was different than before."

"That's the size of it," he said. "It's not bigamy, though. I mean, me and Bonnie aren't married."

"That makes it just fine then," I said.

"No," he said. "It doesn't. I been meaning to get a divorce from your Mama."

"You have to communicate with her for that," I said.

"And I've meant to," Dad said.

"Sounds like you mean to do a lot of things," I said.

"I'm not much good, Dot," Dad said.

"I'll second that," I said.

"But I thought I was dragging you and Frank and your mother down," Dad said. "I thought if I left it would be easier, not harder."

"Oh, come on," I said. "Easier on who? You mean easier on you."

"Maybe so," he said. "I just sort of collapsed. And when I got it back together, I felt it was too late. I didn't know what to say. I didn't know what to do. Things just worked out another way."

"But you have kids," I said, "and I'm one of them. People divorce, but they don't have to divorce the kids."

"I know," he said. "I wish I had some kind of good answer, but I don't."

"Do you ever think about me and Frank at all?" I said.

"Everyday," he said. "I promise. I think about you everyday, and everyday I think should go and try and fix things, but I don't. I don't know why. I just don't. I guess I'm ashamed, and it's been so long now, I don't know what to do."

"Do you love Bonnie and the kid?" I asked.

"I do," he said. "I learned some hard lessons. I'm trying to do right by them."

"Get out and go back to them," I said. "And be sure and treat them better than you did us."

"Dot," he said. "I want to try and make it up to you."

"Get out!" I said. "Get out of my car."

"Okay," he said. "All right."

He opened the door and got out.

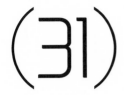

Elbert drove back onto the highway and started us toward home.

"So we aren't kin?" I said.

"We do have the same last name," he said.

"Let me ask it again. We're not kin, right?"

"Right," he said.

"I want to be really mad right now," I said.

"You have every right," he said.

"I do at that," I said, "but you know what? I'm more confused than mad. At Dad, I'm going to be mad."

"You can't do that," he said. "You have to let go of the anger. You don't have to forget, but you have to let it go."

"Thanks," I said. "That fixes me right up. Just tell me why you came to us and parked in our front yard and told us you were our kin."

"Because I wanted to be."

"And you aren't a bank robber," I said. "You're an attempted robber of a beauty parlor."

"Now you're calling me an attempted robber as an insult," he said. "Before, attempted didn't count."

"I thought it was a bank."

"That's why I lied," he said. "Bank robber sounded better. More romantic. More dangerous. I wanted to be interesting."

"Oh, you're interesting, all right."

"I meant in a better way," he said.

"And you weren't in prison?"

"Jail," he said. "For awhile. With your father. You see, we met up, and we sort of drank a little too much, and drinking and desperation, they don't go well together. We decided we'd team up and rob that beauty parlor. Only it didn't work out. We went to jail, and then the lady we tried to rob felt sorry for us, wouldn't press the charges, and she let us out. I asked her for a date. She turned me down."

"Imagine that," I said.

"While I was in jail, your dad and I, we talked. He told me all about you. About his family. I guess he had to tell somebody, and though I wouldn't say we bonded, we were together, and it was on his mind."

"I guess that's something, that we were on his mind," I said. There was a wet drop on my cheek for some reason. I wiped it with my sleeve.

Elbert shifted his eyes toward me. "He said all this good stuff about you, and your mother, your brother, your sister, and yet he walked off. I guess I should add he didn't like your grandmother."

"She saw him for what he was," I said.

"I guess."

"Why would he walk off like that?" I said. "I still don't know even after talking to him. I imagined that day for years. That some day I'd talk to him, and he say something I might not like, but it would be an explanation. He didn't say anything. Not really."

Elbert shook his head. "He told me pretty much what he told you. I don't think he knows why. Not really."

"Can you guess?" I said, and there was catch in my voice. Maybe I was coming down with a cold.

"I think he was scared. I think he ran and didn't know how to go back. Then life changed, and he kept on changing with it. It's no kind of answer, but that's all there is, I think. But I knew, had I ever been fortunate enough to have a family that loved me, I'd have stuck with it. Hell or high water."

"So you decided to borrow one," I said.

"I did. He talked well about you. All of you. I said to him 'You get out of here, go home.' But he wouldn't have it. He said he was through because he had already walked."

"He couldn't walk back?"

"I guess not," Elbert said. "Anyway, we got out of jail and went our own ways. But I kept thinking about your mother and you and your sister and brother. I thought I'd go see you, and tell you your father was fine. That he wasn't dead. That maybe he'd come back. Because, you know, I thought it was possible. Though unlikely. Sometimes, you can just tell someone is done. That they've given up. But, I got there, and your mother and brother and grand-mother were out in the yard, and well…"

"You started lying," I said.

"That's right. And once I told the lie, I couldn't stop lying."

"The clown story?"

"True."

"The roller derby bit?"

"Everything else true. I didn't rob a bank and I didn't go to prison, but the rest of it is true. Well, the parking meter was almost true. I put that in the story because that's where the beauty parlor lady caught up with me the first time she hit me with the hair dryer. I was right by one."

"You're not my uncle," I said.

"And there's that," he said. "Sometimes, though, it's not the blood in the veins that matters, it's the intent in the heart."

"Is that a quote you memorized?" I said.

"Pretty much," he said. "Yeah. I never meant to lie… Well, yeah. I did. But I never meant to hurt anyone. I just wanted to be part of a family. And you're part of a good family."

Joe R. Lansdale

"You think that even after you met us?" I said.

"Yeah," he said. "I do. It's him. Your dad. Not you."

I suppose that was supposed to make me feel better. It didn't. I looked out the windshield. I said, "Just don't talk to me anymore."

We didn't talk after that. I couldn't talk. My throat was too tight. I thought about dad, and how he had been in that yard, ready to mow, and how there was a tricycle in the yard, another kid and a woman in the house. How he had a job and was maintaining. And yet, me and my family, his own blood, we weren't enough.

When we got back to Marvel Creek and pulled into the mobile home park, Elbert pulled up in front of our house and gave me the keys to my car.

He said, "I'm sorry."

I didn't say anything to that. I slid over to the driver's seat, put the keys in, backed out and left him there in the yard, watching me go away.

I drove around for awhile. Then I drove out to the hill where I had freaked on Herb. I sat there for a long time and watched the night crawl down from the daylight like a cat from a tree. The night was starless because it was still full of rain clouds. I sat there a long time. Finally a car parked near me, and that was my cue. I started up the car and drove around some more, and then finally back to the house.

It was late when I got there.

T *he world seemed to* tilt as I walked into the trailer. When
I did the light came on over the kitchen table. Mom was
sitting there in her flannel night gown, her hand on the wall light
switch. I could see Frank asleep on the couch, covered up in light
blanket, a teddy bear for a pillow.

"You're late," Mom said. She said it softly, but there was an
edge to her voice that you could have used to open envelopes.

I crutched over to the table, sat down, poked my injured foot
out in front of me.

"I know," I said.

"And the reason is?"

I paused for a moment. And I won't kid you, I started to
lie. I didn't want to tell her where I had gone or who I had seen,
because at first I thought it would just make her feel worse. But
that wasn't fair. She deserved to know what I knew.

"I saw Dad," I said.

It was like the oxygen got sucked out of the room. I could
hear the light thumping of the battery-powered clock on the wall
near the kitchen sink. I could hear myself breathe.

"You actually saw him," Mom finally said.

"Yeah."

She nodded. She got up and went to the refrigerator and
pulled out a large bottle of cheap soda and got a couple of glasses
out of the cabinet and brought it all back to the table. As solemn

as she was, you would have thought she had pulled down a bottle of whisky.

She sat down and opened the soda and poured us both a glass. She carefully put the lid on the bottle. It was like a ritual. I had seen her do it before. She got nervous, worried, she went for the big soda. It was one way I knew the bills were overdue or that maybe a piece of furniture was going to be repossessed, or we had had to let the layaway go back.

"What did he have to say?" she asked.

"Well, he's sorry. He has a new home and family. He's not coming back. And he hasn't got enough sense not to mow a yard when the grass is wet. That's pretty much it."

"To the point," Mama said.

"Yep," I said. "It was pretty direct. And the good stuff just keeps on coming. He was in jail. And Elbert isn't any kin to us at all."

"Figures," Mama said. "Typical. Perfect. I really liked him."

I told her about the whole trip in detail. What Dad had said, what Elbert had said.

When I was finished, Mama said, "You know, when I was a girl, I wanted to be a princess, marry Prince Charming. Later I just wanted to have a job and someone to come home to that would be here and at least wasn't a frog, and if things were really working right, they'd have a job too. Hell, maybe even a good-natured frog with a job would be okay. I didn't picture myself at my age living in a trailer wearing a flannel nightgown wondering where my husband had gone, then finding out he had gone about an hour or so away and wasn't coming back."

Her eyes had tears. I reached out took hold of her hand. "You've done all right by us, Mama."

"Sure," she said. "We're living in the lap of luxury."

"We're together," I said.

"Elbert actually thought we were a good family?" she said.

"Yeah," I said. "He envied us. Wanted to be a part of it."

"Even after meeting us?" Mama said, giving me a smile so weak I thought it would fall off her mouth.

"What I said, and he said yes, even after meeting us."

"If that ain't something," she said.

When I crawled into bed, I could hear Grandma snoring like a chainsaw cutting up lumber. I lay there and listened to her for a long time. I was worn out, and yet I couldn't sleep. It was like there were needles in my brain, and every time I started to drift off, they poked me and woke me up. I tried to come up with a good dream to sleep by, but when I got one started, I would come awake again.

It began to rain. It wasn't a hammering rain, but it was a brisk rain. It hit the roof of the trailer and there was a rhythm about it. A soft, steady rain helps me sleep sometime, but not this night, not this hard, mean rain.

I lay there confused, but in some way, oddly satisfied. I hadn't felt all that satisfied just moments before, but after talking to Mama I did. After thinking about all she had done, all she had given up to hold the family together, I felt different.

I wasn't happy at what I had found out, or hadn't found out, as Dad hadn't exactly been crystal clear as to why he had done what he had done. But a short time earlier I had felt as bad as I had ever felt, like I was lost in a great woods and it was full of hungry animals and I was what they wanted for dinner.

But as I lay there, listening to the rain, I realized that life wasn't always a bed of roses for anyone. Or maybe it was more like you had to realize that the roses had thorns. You could pay all your attention to the thorns and hate the roses, or you could give them a wider look. See how pretty they were, how good they smelled.

And maybe I was so tired I was delirious.

I listened to the rain with my eyes open, staring up at the roof, trying to imagine that I was able to see through it, see out into the night sky full of rain. I tried to imagine it washing away everything that bothered me. This time the trick worked and the hard sound of the rain didn't bother me anymore. I finally fell asleep.

When I got up in the morning, I could hear the TV going faintly in the living room. I rolled out of bed slowly, and found I could stand on my foot without the crutches. I glanced at the clock. It was ten o'clock. I limped to the window and looked outside.

Elbert's van was gone.

(34)

I walked carefully, so as not to put too much weight on my foot. The swelling was gone, and there was just a sharp pain from time to time. It made me feel a little more optimistic. Last night, as I drifted off, I had felt really good for a while, and I was afraid all of that would be gone when I got up. Some of it was, but there was a bit of it left, like milk on my lips.

In the kitchen Grandma was sitting on the couch watching TV.

"About time you got up," she said. "Me, I was up at six a.m."

"So you could sit on the couch and watch TV?" I said. "I'm not sure what the rush is."

"Well, your mother got up early and went to work," she said.

"I'm off work," I said. "Injured."

"In my day we worked no matter what," she said. "I had been you, at your age, I'd have been working on crutches."

"Thank goodness you're making up for all that hard work now by sitting on the couch," I said. "Where's Frank?"

"Bible camp," she said.

"Like he's read it," I said.

"Read what?"

"The Bible," I said.

"Well," Grandma said, "at least the little turd is gone for a week."

I went in the kitchen and filled myself a bowl of cereal. I got the milk out.

"That was a good thing you did?" Grandma said.

"What?" I said.

"Your Dad. Finding him like that."

"I don't know how good it was," I said.

"I think it made your Mama feel better to just know he wasn't dead and rotting in a ditch somewhere. I was kind of hoping for that, but I'll settle just knowing he was as sorry as I thought he was."

"That's so nice of you," I said. "You should write greeting cards."

"It's the spelling that gives me a problem," she said.

I poured milk into my cereal bowl and sat at the table. I was finishing it up when there was a knock on the door.

"You better get that," Grandma said, not moving anything but her mouth.

I went to the door, and when I opened it, there was Herb.

"Oh," I said.

"Good morning," he said.

I hadn't even looked in the mirror, but I had an idea I wasn't exactly aces. The fact that he looked like a doll didn't help my feelings much. If his clothes had been any crisper you could have used the crease in his pants to shave with. Not that I need to shave, though I do have this one pesky chin hair I have to work on with tweezers now and then.

"We can talk here in the doorway, or you can come outside, or maybe you'll invite me inside," he said.

I turned and looked back at Grandma, lounging on the couch like a bear. When I looked back at Herb, I eased out the door and closed it. "Let's sit in lawn chairs."

The lawn chairs had turned over in the night and they were damp with rain, so we went and sat in my car instead, me behind the wheel, Herb in the passenger seat.

"I've been calling you," he said.

"My phone is dead," I said. "I'm out of minutes. I told you about it."

He nodded. "I forgot. Look, I can help you out there."

"No thanks," I said.

"That's your pride again," he said.

"It's one thing I've kept," I said, "though right now it, like my foot, has a limp."

"I just want to talk to you," he said.

"And I want to talk to you," I said. "But I don't want charity."

"All right," he said. "All right." He looked at my foot. "You going to be able to skate?"

"Another day or two I should be back to work."

"I mean in the derby."

"You have been talking to Bob," I said.

"And the other girls," he said. "They all want to try it."

"It was a stupid idea," I said. "No way a handful of small town girls who skate at a drive-through are going to beat a team of professionals."

"Maybe," he said. "But do you have to beat them for it to matter?"

"I think so," I said. "Yeah, I think we do."

"Doesn't it matter that you try and beat them?"

I thought about that. "I don't know. Does it?"

"I can't answer that for you," he said. "It would mean something to those girls. They think of you as their leader."

"They do?"

"Even your sister. They think you're coming back on fire and they're going to take it to those derby girls."

"They do, huh?"

"They do," Herb said. "Well, maybe not Gay."

"Of course not Gay," I said. "I just got their hopes up. I don't know what I was thinking."

"You were thinking you wanted to matter," Herb said.

"That's it, huh?"

"From what you told me. Yeah. That's what I think."

He studied my face for a long while. I feared it might be that pesky chin hair I told you about.

Leaning forward, he kissed me lightly on the lips. I didn't fight.

"I haven't brushed my teeth," I said.

"You tasted pretty sweet to me," he said.

"Yeah," I said, and leaned forward and we kissed again.

"Okay," he said, "maybe some toothpaste wouldn't hurt."

We laughed.

The next few days I tried to exercise my ankle, sitting on the bed, flexing it, turning my toes first to the right, then the left. I went for short walks, and I tried on the skates.

They were new skates. Herb bought them for me. I didn't like that at first, but he said they were for my birthday. It wasn't my birthday, but what the heck. I took them with the idea that maybe I could get back to work. I needed the money

As for the derby, well, I hadn't seen any of the girls. For some reason, I didn't really want to see any of them. What I had found out about my father seemed to me like it had left a sentence written across my forehead that said: My daddy dumped me and got a new and better family.

I went out and skated along the trailer park drive. I skated up and down it, carrying a dog stick with me. I skated up and down that drive so much the dogs stopped barking at me after the third day. I stopped carrying the stick. I started skating for speed. My ankle was strong. I felt strong. Out there on the wheels, the wind blowing on me, I felt swift and powerful. I might not play in a roller derby, but at least I had those moments going for me.

On the third day I was skating, when I turned and came back to our trailer, Elbert's van was parked in the yard. He was leaning against the front of it. Herb's car was parked in the yard too, and Herb was standing outside of it, leaning on his fender. They looked like two hit men waiting for me.

As I skated up, out of Elbert's van, stepped Raylynn, Sue, Gay and Miranda. They all went around to stand near Elbert. Except Herb. He stayed at his car. I had a car like that, I'd stay with it too.

When I stopped skating between van and car, I said, "Who's minding the store?"

"Bob and a couple of new girls," Raylynn said.

"What are you goobers doing?" I asked.

"We're here to kidnap you," Raylynn said.

"We'll grab you and take you away if we have to," Sue said.

"I'll just watch," Gay said. "I'm not getting in on that."

"What are you meatheads talking about?" I said.

"You," Raylynn said.

"You got our hopes up and said we should go after those roller derby girls. That we should try and win that money."

"I was out of my mind," I said.

"You said it," Sue said, "and we believed it."

"That you could win?" I said.

"Maybe not that we could win," Raylynn said, "but that we mattered. That all of us mattered. We had just been hanging around, like fruit rotting on a limb, and then you gave us hope."

"What hope?" I said. "That you might get picked fresh?"

"Okay," Sue said, "the fruit thing maybe doesn't work, but the truth is you gave us hope, and now you're taking it away."

"How am I taking anything?" I looked at Elbert. "He put you up to this." I turned and looked at Herb. "Or him. One kiss, and now he's running my life."

"Two kisses," Herb said, "and your teeth weren't brushed."

"They been training," Elbert said. "Bob has been giving them time off, and I been helping them."

"You girls do know he was a skating clown," I said, pointing at Elbert.

"We do," Raylynn said, "and I know he's no kin to me and you. But we also know he was in the derby, and he can skate, and he's been teaching us. In fact, right now, I think we wanted, way we been training, we could hand you your head."

"You think so, huh?"

"Oh yeah," Sue said.

"Big time," Miranda said.

"I am at the top of my game," Raylynn said.

"That might be a short climb," I said.

"Proof is in the pudding," Gay said. Then: "Sorry, that just popped out. I'm not even really sure what that means. My mother says it."

"It means that you can talk a good pudding," Raylynn said, "but that the proof is in the pudding itself."

"So I'm a pudding now," I said.

"No," Miranda said. "You're our jammer."

The girls and Elbert piled into the van, and me and Herb rode in his car. We followed the van. It came to the skating rink. Or what used to be the skating rink. It was closed as of recent.

When we got out of the van and car, the girls all had their skates thrown over their shoulders. I had mine with me. Before we left I took them off and put on my tennis shoes. I said, "Why here?"

"It's a skating rink, isn't it," Elbert said, then looked at me in a nervous way. I wasn't sure how mad I still was at him. Truth was I kind of missed him being out there in the yard in his lawn chair.

"This isn't some kind of criminal thing," I said. "I mean, we're not breaking into this place on your word, and later we're all in the Big House, or busting rocks while wearing striped suits."

"Bob got permission for us," Raylynn said, as we moved toward the door. "He knew somebody that knew somebody."

Elbert took out a key and unlocked the door to the rink. Inside the place smelled of dust, and the dust moved in the air like insects. There was another smell too. One I can't describe. But it smelled like when I was younger and learning to skate here. It smelled like when my Dad brought me here and held me up while I skated. It smelled like the times Raylynn and I had skated here together, and it smelled like the time we got in a fist fight over cotton candy. I won the fight. But the pink wisp of candy in a cone fell on the floor and neither one of us ate it. Dad refused to buy us another.

Inside there was a bench row where you could sit and put on your skates. The girls sat and put on their skates. I put on mine too.

Herb said, "Don't overdo that ankle."

Elbert put on his skates. There was a little bar of a door that led to the rink. He pushed it back and went out on his skates and started skating. He went forward awhile, then in reverse. I figured long as he didn't try to jump something backwards, he was okay.

The girls went out on their skates. I sat where I was, tying mine into place.

"You just wait here," Raylynn said. "Let us show you what we got."

She nearly slipped down going through the gate, but I pretended not to notice.

When she and the other girls were out on the rink, they started skating, all of them very fast. They did this for awhile, and then they banded together and started to skate. They were really moving, and they were moving well.

"Did you know about all this all the time, Herb?"

"No," he said. "I found out about it lately."

"But you're in on this?"

"You started something you need to finish. I don't want to meddle, but from what you've told me, and forgive me for saying it, the big problem with your family is no one gets the chance to finish something, or they chose not to finish it. You finish this, you can finish other things."

"That rich boy advice?" I said.

His face twisted, and I was sorry I had said it. My mouth sometimes writes checks it hates to cash.

"Before you jump on me, I'm using your own concerns to say if you finish this, you can finish other things. A high school education. Going to college. And while I'm catching flak from you,

I'm going to throw this out there too. Elbert might be a whole lot more all right than you give him credit for. Come to think of, you don't give anyone credit for much. Not even yourself."

"All right," I said, "that's going to hold me today as far as philosophy goes."

I got up and cautiously moved across the wooden floor to the gate.

"Break a leg," Herb said.

I put my hand on the gate and turned to look at Herbert. "I already have a sprained ankle, thank you very much," I said.

"It's a theater term for do well," he said.

"This isn't the theater," I said.

"All right, then," he said. "Skate pretty."

I grinned at him and went through the gate and onto the rink. As soon as I started to roll out there, I felt like a different person, way I had felt earlier. I didn't feel any pain in my ankle. I wasn't even aware of my legs. They worked without me thinking about it. On wheels I was not of this earth.

I turned and skated backwards the way Elbert had, the way he had taught me. I skated past him, going the opposite direction. He smiled at me. I smiled back.

(37)

Bob wanted his skaters to win. I think it wasn't just because he liked roller derby. I think he saw it as advertisement. He said he was going to get us shirts that said DAIRY BOB on the back. We told him no. We wanted them to say FENDER LIZARDS.

"All right," Bob said. We were all inside the Dairy Bob, sitting in customer booths, except Bob, who was leaning on the counter. "I can live with that, but somehow we have to tie it into the Dairy Bob. I'm going to have to work for you girls, me and the manager, which, face it, is my cousin and not that good a worker, then I've got to get some kind of advertisement."

"We'll figure something out," Raylynn said.

We talked about it some more, and then Elbert took us to the rink and we trained. Afterwards, we went to the Dairy Bob and did short shifts, went home to dinner and rested up, started all over the next day.

We usually trained mornings. Sometimes all of the girls couldn't be there, but mostly we were all together. After a time, Elbert quit concentrating on how to skate, and started concentrating on the game of roller derby itself. He started to act and sound like a coach. He even got himself a whistle on a chain to wear around his neck. He wore shorts and tennis shoes when he didn't have on his skates.

One morning he had us all out on the rink in our skates. He said, "Okay, you're skating good. All of you. Now you need to really know how to play the game. What I'm going to do is I'm going to assign positions. Dot, we all know you're our jammer."

"Is there a reason you chose me for that job?" I said.

"Yes," Miranda said, "you beat a guy up with a board."

"That's it?" I said.

"It was the only thing we could think up as a requirement," Sue said. "We thought maybe dolling down the catwalk, but that would have been Gay. It didn't seem to go with roller derby. We needed someone with Neanderthal blood."

"Okay," I said. "You've had your fun. I'm the jammer."

"Good," Elbert said. "Now everyone else is a blocker. We don't have backup, so if one of you gets a leg broke or dies, that just leaves four, and so on. I figure we get down to three we have to forfeit. It also makes it hard to train, because we don't have a team to play against. I'll try and figure something for that in the next day or two. Way we'll work it for now is three of you will be the opposing team, and two of you will be our team."

"That sucks," Sue said.

"It does," Elbert said, "but there you have it. Okay, we can do this. I'll also be on a team. So we got three and three. I'll mainly just show you the ropes as I go. I won't be hitting."

"Hitting?" Gay said.

"There's some contact," Elbert said.

"How much contact?" Gay said.

"Oh, it's not that bad," Elbert said.

So we ran plays. My job was pretty simple. I was the jammer. I ran against the other team's jammer. Jammers were put in the back. It was simply a game of the jammer passing the other team's players without being stopped, and your players keeping them from stopping you.

We played tag at first, because that's the way Elbert showed us. It was polite. We tagged each other as we passed by patting the other girls on the shoulder as we went. After awhile Elbert had us try to skate in such a way we couldn't be tagged.

Then he explained we could use our hips and shoulders to bump our opponents out of the way. We did that for awhile. Then he told us the other team might do a little more than that.

He was explaining all this as he skated with us.

Gay squealed her skates to a stop when he said that part about what the other team might do. She said, "How much are they going to hit?"

"Well, they might use their elbows," he said. "They're not supposed to do that in a really bad way, but they will. So you have to do it back."

"Are we talking to the face?" Gay said.

"They could get disqualified for that," Elbert said.

"But they might do it anyway?" Gay asked.

"Yes," he said.

"We could get hurt," Gay said.

"Yes, you could," Elbert said. "So you have to skate a lot faster and you have to hit a lot harder. Mostly I'd advise skating faster and using avoidance maneuvers."

"Is it too late to back out?" Gay said.

"We're not going to," Raylynn said. "Or at least I'm not."

"One for one," I said, "and one for all."

I stuck out my hand.

"What's that mean?" Gay said.

"It means we're all on the same side, and that we're all for each other," Raylynn said. She put her hand on top of mine.

Then Sue and Miranda put theirs on the pile.

Gay said, "My Mama says y'all are bad influences."

"She may be right," I said.

Gay chewed her bottom lip a moment, then moved forward and placed her hand on top. Her nails were perfect.

Elbert placed his on top of ours.

"One for one," he said, and then we all said, "and one for all."

Next day we went to the skating rink. Elbert was already there with his skates on and a clown costume. There were a number of cub scouts in their uniforms with skates on. I guess they were nine or ten. There was a fat man in a scout uniform with a cap that fit him the way a thimble would fit a bear's head. He looked nervous. He didn't have on skates.

Elbert skated over to me. "I talked the local Cub Scout Master into having his kids come skate for fun, and to be kind of your opponents."

"They're children," Raylynn said.

"That will make you look better," Elbert said. "Besides, it's what we got."

"Why are you wearing a clown suit," I asked.

"I don't get many chances to wear it," he said. "The Cub Scouts love it."

I looked out at them. They didn't seem all that loving. In fact, for nine and ten year olds they looked kind of surly.

"It's going to be hard to take orders from a clown with a whistle," I said.

"You'll manage," he said.

Way it worked was Elbert had the Scouts skate, we tried to pass between them, and they tried to get in front of us. Every time they blocked us or kept me from passing one of them, Elbert would mark on a wash-and erase board he was carrying. Their prize at the end of the day was drinks, fries and hamburgers supplied by the Dairy Bob.

This was our training.

It was kind of like learning to ride broncos by using a stick horse. By the middle of the day there were a lot of marks on that board against us, but by the end of the day, we were doing better.

Finished up, I went home and wrote out a couple of invitations. One was to High Top. It read:

> Miss High Top. I hope you remember me. My name is Dot. I helped take care of the dogs because I was briefly a criminal. I also came out and took care of them just because I wanted to. But that's not what this note is about. I'm skating in a roller derby, and I'd like to invite you to come see me. I won't cry if you don't come, but I'll be sad a little, and inwardly I will be crushed and never be quite the same again. It would be great if you could be there. The dogs are invited, but I think it best they don't come. I don't think there are enough seats. If I don't get killed at the derby, then maybe you could start helping me study for the GED like you offered.

I put the date and location on it, sealed it up and put a stamp on it. I wrote another.

> Mr. Sherman: You may remember me because I saw you just the other day. I am your daughter. You have two more children and a wife you need to divorce. I am skating in a roller derby. I am a jammer. I guess I'm inviting you to come see me. You don't need to, and if you do, you don't need to make anything out of it. But I think I should invite you because that's what daughters do. If

you plan to smoke, please buy smokes before you come, as I know how easy it is for you to get lost if you go shopping. As an added note, Bonnie and your new child are not invited. I'm not ready for that yet. Here's a tip I thought I'd provide, because it's obvious you don't know it. Don't try and mow wet grass. It bunches up on the mower blade and causes the thing to jam up.

I gave him the time and location.

I carried both letters out to the mailbox and put up the flag. I went in the house, hung around awhile, and considered removing the letter to my dad. By the time I decided that's what I was going to do, the mail lady had come and the mail was gone.

ay before the derby, me and Elbert went to the carnival. It was set up and was already doing business. It was pretty small and had a desperate feel about it. We went over and found the guy who owned it. He was a big fellow that had a trailer on the lot where the carnival was. It was a little trailer, fastened to the back of a large, blue truck with big tires.

We knocked on the trailer door. A man in a light blue cowboy suit, kind of thing with upside down triangles stitched above the pockets, opened the door. He was also wearing a big white cowboy hat, and boots that had toes so thin and long and sharp, he could have kicked a cockroach to death in the corner of a room. He had a belly like a watermelon under his shirt.

"Yeah," he said.

Elbert stuck out his hand. "Elbert."

The cowboy looked at Elbert's hand, took it as if he might be shaking the tail of a mackerel.

"What can I do for you?" the cowboy said.

"You're Mr. Wilkin?"

"Yeah."

"We want to sign up for the roller derby."

"Ah," said Wilkin. "Come inside."

It was small inside, but it was well arranged. There was a table that fastened to the wall and could be pushed up and locked into place. Mr. Wilkin unfastened it and lowered it. There was a booth on one side of it. He had a stool too. I could see through an open door at the back that there was a bed. There were carnival posters on the wall.

"Sit down right there," he said. He looked at me. "This one of your roller girls?"

"Yes," said Elbert. "She's our jammer."

"Looks a little puny," he said.

"She'll stand up to it all right," Elbert said.

"Well," said Mr. Wilkin, "I got a contract here. Way it works, your team skates against ours, we'll give them five thousand dollars if they win."

"The poster says ten," Elbert said.

"Yeah, well, I exaggerated because they're hardly any towns that have roller derby teams."

"It says ten," Elbert said, "and we want ten."

"I'm giving five," Mr. Wilkin said.

"Here's the thing," Elbert said. "The sheriff in this town is a good friend of mine. What you're offering on your poster is false advertising. You look like a man might have spent some time in jail, so do you want to spend more?"

This was going ugly quick. And Elbert was lying through his teeth, though he might be able to recognize jail birds from personal experience.

"I could just cancel the whole event," Mr. Wilkin said. "Say one of the girls got a sprained ankle. Maybe it's going around."

"A sprained ankle?" I said.

"Make it measles then," Mr. Wilkin said.

"I could also spread around you chickened out of the challenge, and that sheriff I know might not mind closing you down for some kind of violation. I thought one of those wires grounding the tilt-a-whirl looked a little loose."

"Hasn't broken in months," Mr. Wilkin said.

"Look," Elbert said. "We come here to sign up, like your poster says. That's it. Play fair."

"Life ain't fair," Mr. Wilkin said.

"Today it can be," Elbert said.

Mr. Wilkin pursed his lips, placed his hands on his watermelon belly. "All right," he said. "Tell you what. We normally have our own team that plays the other. That way we always got a challenger. We sometimes say they're from the town next to the one where we are, just to make things a little more local. Give the rubes someone to root for, then our team wins."

"Because it's rigged," Elbert said.

"Because it's a game, not a sport; it's like professional wrestling. But the thing is I don't have a spare team anymore. This roller derby thing, it's not the big event it used to be. So, if you want to be the hometown team, that's all right, but if you're the hometown team, how about you play the best you can, and then throw it a little?"

"Fake a loss?" Elbert said.

"That's right," Mr. Wilkin said.

"You fake a loss, I give you two thousand dollars for your team," Mr. Wilkin said. "And I'll throw in fifty dollars for you personally as manager, and free tickets for everyone to the carnival. That way you all make some money, and I'm not out so much. Course, if you go straight, play us and lose, well, you get nothing."

"But if we win?" I said.

"You won't," he said. "I got the best team there is."

"So why make the offer?" Elbert said.

"Because a good team can have a night off," he said, "and a night off could cost me five thousand dollars."

"Ten," Elbert said.

"All right then," Wilkins said. "Ten. But the way I'm talking, you and your team get a payday, and I keep most of what I'd pay out if you won. Thing is, though, I can be reasonably certain we'll win, and you won't get money. Also, there's a hundred dollar entry fee. So you see I'm throwing you a bone with some meat still on it."

Elbert studied Mr. Wilkin a long time. Neither of them blinked. "All right," Elbert said. He lifted his butt and took out his billfold, peeled some money out of it. Five twenties.

"There's the entry fee," Elbert said, "but we're not throwing any game."

"That's actually the best choice for me," Mr. Wilkin said. "That way, when my girls run over yours like road kill, I won't be out nothing, and you'll be as humiliated as if you all showed up to play in your boxer shorts and nothing else."

"We're girls," I said. "We don't wear boxer shorts. Least I don't."

"Whatever your undergarment situation," Mr. Wilkin said. "It's on now. I offered you a way out to save a little face, have my girls give you a little room, play light, let you go home with some money and all your teeth. But you bailed on that idea."

"We wouldn't have it any other way," Elbert said.

Mr. Wilkin nodded. "Good. I'll get a contract."

On the way out to the car, Elbert, carrying our copy of the contract said, "I just talked you girls out of two thousand dollars, and me out of fifty dollars."

"Don't forget the carnival tickets," I said. "And if we had pushed, we might have gotten some free cotton candy."

"It is just an entertainment, not a true sport," Elbert said. "We could probably go back and change the deal."

"Now, now," I said. "That's the beauty parlor robber and the liar talking."

"Attempted beauty parlor robber," he said.

"Elbert, I noticed on the contract it said everyone needed to be eighteen or older. Some of the girls are, but some are not. I would be in the 'are not' category."

"I know that," he said, "and I hesitated to sign. I decided a carnival like this isn't going to check birth certificates. Just promise me you won't get killed, because if you do, until my dying day, I'll say you forged my name to that contract, and you won't be here to contradict me."

"I promise," I said.

When we got to my car, I paused at the hood of it, looked at Elbert. "Way I see it, if I can go out there, if all us girls can go out there, give it all we got, it'll make us feel like we're not just hanging out until we get knocked up. Except for Gay, of course. She won't be hanging around at all."

"You want to be like Rocky, show you're not just another bum in the neighborhood," Elbert said.

"That the movie about the boxer?" I said.

"Yep."

"Okay," I said, moving around to the driver's side of the car, "that's what I want. To be like Rocky, show I'm not just another bum in the neighborhood. Course, if we lose, maybe I'll wish we took the deal."

"I hear that," Elbert said, climbing inside the car.

When I was sitting behind the wheel, and Elbert was in his seat, I said, "You know what really worries me?"

"What?" Elbert said.

"We've never actually played against anyone but some Cub Scouts."

"I have a similar concern," Elbert said.

(41)

That night we met at the Dairy Bob. Bob had hired a few more part-time girls to skate, and had even hired a guy as well. He wasn't being the sexist Bob I knew and loved so well, which meant, of course, he was desperate.

There were two women there waiting on us. They were wearing shorts and halter tops. They were nice looking girls, but older than us, maybe by five years. One was sitting on the counter chewing gum. Bob never let anyone sit on the counter, but he didn't say anything to this girl. She was dark haired and strong looking, like she could tie a tire iron in a knot. The other girl was dishwater blonde, tall, well over six foot, and because of that she looked thin, but wasn't. She was muscular. She was leaning against the wall like she was waiting for something to come by that she could kill and eat. Between them, they had enough tattoos for the entire U.S. Navy and about half the Coast Guard and a biker club.

Elbert was there with us. The Dairy Bob was closed. It never closed, so that was odd unto itself. The lights were off outside. A car came up and circled, parked, and sat there. Bob went out and said something to them and they went away.

While he was outside we looked at the two new girls, and they looked at us. They made me want to look away.

When Bob came back in, he went to one of the boxes and opened it. He pulled out new head gear, shin guards, elbow pads.

"This here stuff will keep you from getting hurt," he said. "It's better than that stuff you got."

"Promise?" said Gay.

"I guess I ought to say it will keep you from getting hurt as bad as you might," Bob said.

"Not what I wanted to hear," Gay said.

He took out an example of each. He said, "There ought to be all the right sizes. When it's all over, I want this stuff back."

"What, we can't wear it to the shopping mall or on dates?" Sue said.

"Funny," Bob said.

He opened the other box. He pulled out some very green tee-shirts with yellow letters that read: FENDER LIZARDS. Below that in slightly smaller letters were the words: Eat at the Dairy Bob.

"That's our colors," he said. "Green and yellow. The carnival team, if I have the right information, wears red and black."

"Red for the blood of their enemies," said Raylynn, "black for the color of their hearts."

"That's about right," said the tall girl in the corner.

We all looked at her.

"Did these girls come out of a box too?" I asked.

"These two ladies," Bob said, "are what you call ringers. Meaning they actually know how to play the game. They were with an Austin league that went out of business."

"Did you not win enough?" Sue said to the tall girl.

"Unsportsmanlike behavior," said the tall girl. "Excessive force."

"Oh," Sue said.

"I read about them online," Bob said. "I'm paying them a salary for playing with you girls. They don't get a slice of the prize should you win."

"Good luck with that," said the girl on the counter. "These girls you'll be playing, they used to be a real league. We've played with some of them when they were out of Austin too. Thing is, not enough roller derby fans, so they had to go to work with the carnival."

"If we can't win," Gay said, "what's the point?"

"You play because you can," the tall girl said. "You play because in that moment when you're out there, and you got true competition, it's pretty rad."

"Okay," I said. "Okay. You know, we really don't know how to play this game. We know the rules, but we've mostly been training against Cub Scouts."

"That's why we're here," the tall one said. "They call me Lightning Strike. This here," she motioned toward the dark-haired girl, "is Thunder Bomb."

"Your mothers certainly had interesting ideas for names," Gay said.

"Those are our handles for roller derby," Thunder Bomb said, glaring at Gay, who stepped back a couple of steps, "and they'll do."

"Certainly," I said.

"We're all fine with that," Elbert said.

"What we're going to do," Lightning Strike said, "is we're going to go to that roller rink, and we're going to cram, so that tomorrow night, right before you lose, they will think maybe you actually had done this a time or two."

"Tonight," Gay said.

"Yeah," Bob said, "tonight. I got all kind of money tied up in this. It could be great for business."

"And the girls wear shorts," I said.

"There's that," he said.

(42)

It was rougher than the Cub Scouts. Lightning Strike and Thunder Bomb couldn't skate any faster than us, or maybe not any better, but they could skate more sneaky-like. They could look like they were going to do one thing, then they'd do the other.

Way they set it up was the five of us were to skate around them. We couldn't, not at first. They hit us with elbows, tripped us, bounced their hips against us and sent us flying. I was glad I had on all that armor and a mouthpiece.

Gay got elbowed into the center of the rink where Elbert, serving as coach and referee, sat in a chair. It was a good blow and sent her rolling, throwing her mouthpiece to the sky. When she came up on her feet she was holding her jaw. She yelled, "That's got to be against the rules."

Thunder Bomb, who was skating past when Gay called out, spun on her skate, gliding right up against Gay. She stuck her nose against Gay's nose. I stopped and watched.

"Yeah, what rules there are," Thunder Bomb said, "I guess that's against it. If you get caught, or the referee decides to say something."

Thunder Bomb looked at Elbert.

"Didn't see a thing," Elbert said.

"What?" Gay said. "If she'd knocked me any harder or higher, I'd have had been served peanuts on that flight."

Elbert shrugged.

"Roller derby is played to be rough," Thunder Bomb said.

By this time Lightning Strike had skated up too. We all had. Lightning Strike skated up close to Gay.

"Rules are made to be broken," Lightning Strike said. "Like bones."

I glide in close then. "But not our bones," I said. "Gay is our teammate, and you will play less rough."

"Yeah," said Lightning Strike. She gave me a look that curled the hairs in my nose.

"Yeah," I said. It came out more like a cough.

Lightning Strike grinned. "Now you're learning. Team work. It's all about the team. You understand? You protect your team. Now, all of you get back on the track so I can run you over."

"What happened to it's all about the team?" I said.

Lightning Strike and Thunder Bomb grinned.

"Do that to me again," Gay said to Thunder Bomb, "and I will hit you so hard they'll find your body when they first put a human on Mars."

"That's right," Thunder Bomb said. "Get tough."

Thunder Bomb turned and started skating around the rink.

Gay looked at me. "I shouldn't have said that about hitting her, should I?"

"I don't blame you," I said.

"Yeah, but now I'm scared to get back on the track," Gay said. "She has a mean streak."

"Your choice," I said. "But me, I'm out to win this thing."

I got back on the track and started skating. When I looked over my shoulder, Gay was skating after me, pushing her mouthpiece into place.

It was maybe three in the morning when we quit. We ran all manner of drills. We even managed to get by Thunder Bomb and Lightning Strike a few times, the result being only some black eyes and bruises and a darker view of humanity.

Out in the lot as I was loading my gear into the car, I saw Elbert walking toward his van. I went over to him.

"I'm glad you didn't go," I said.

"Thanks," he said. "You mean it?"

"I appreciate what you're doing, but I still think pretending to be my uncle was a dirty trick," I said.

Elbert nodded. "It was."

"But I'm glad you did it," I said.

"You know what," Elbert said. "Me too."

"Where you staying?" I said.

"In the van, as always," he said.

"Do you want to park in our yard?"

"Does your mother know about me?"

"Yep."

"Is she mad?"

"Yep," I said. "She is. But you know what?"

"What?" he said.

"It'll pass."

When *I woke up* the next morning, I felt as if I had been folded and stuffed in a space too small. I could hardly get out of bed. Grandma had already abandoned the room. I got up and went to the bathroom and took a long hot shower. That loosened me up some.

Dressed, I went to the kitchen. I was surprised to see Mama and Grandma and Frank all sitting together with Elbert at the table.

I said, "Mama, what you doing off work?"

"It's my day off," she said. "Now and again they give me one, and all I have to do on that day is feel guilty. It's what they expect."

"Oh," I said. "Yeah, okay. I haven't been keeping up."

Frank looked at me. He said, "Elbert says you're going to kick some ass tonight."

"Don't talk like that," Mama said.

"You're gonna lose some teeth, is what I figure," Grandma said.

"Thanks, Grandma," I said. "Thanks for the support."

"Just saying," she said.

"Me and your mother," Elbert said, "we been talking. I like to think she understands where I'm coming from, why I did what I did."

"I do," said Mama to Elbert, "but I still don't like it. That said, I forgive you."

She looked at Elbert and smiled. And I knew something then. She liked him, and not just as a relative. It was kind of shocking that I was just now noticing it. I think it had been in the air all along, but she had thought of him as her husband's brother, now that she knew he wasn't and Dad wasn't coming back... Well, she had a different outlook. I could see it in her eyes. I almost laughed. I wasn't sure if I liked it, or if the idea made me a little ill.

I looked at Frank. "How was Bible Camp?"

"It was all right," he said.

"You're going to need to eat a hearty breakfast, Dot," Mama said. "A decent lunch, and a light supper. I'll bring some snacks for you and the girls."

"You're going to watch?" I said.

"We all are," Mama said.

"Even you, Grandma?" I asked.

"Might as well," Grandma said. "TV isn't that good tonight. But I figure I won't like it. Just warning you. The only sport I like is horseshoes."

"I consider myself warned," I said.

"You sit down," Mama said. "Today I'm going to fix you breakfast, and you're going to take it easy and relax."

"All right," I said.

I sat down. I looked at Elbert. He looked at me, and slowly smiled.

(44)

ime came.
It was a bright night, the stars as sharp as pin-points. The sky looked soft as a kitten's fur. The moon was full. We were inside a big circus tent, but for some reason it was wide open at the peak, a large flap thrown back, and the stars and the moon seemed to be falling through the opening.

I was on my skates, standing in the center of the rink, looking up, perhaps hoping for divine help. I looked down, studied the rink. It was a more rickety rink than the one we had been practicing on. It moved when you moved. It squeaked like a mouse and groaned like a bear. It had a collision rail all around it, and the rail was wrapped in padding and the padding was wrapped with duct tape. The railing looked well used, like many a body had been thrown against it. The center was open and the ground was visible. There was a big canister of Gator Aid on a table at both ends of the opening; one for each team. There were benches and chairs for both teams when we took a break.

What astounded me was how full the stands were; Elbert said it was because a lot of the people followed the team. That some of them had come from as far as Amarillo. I could see people holding pink, spun cotton candy, popcorn bags, peanuts, and there was the noise of candy boxes being shook and feet being shuffled, and people talking and laughing. Straws sucked at sodas. Young children cried or laughed, or just made noise to hear their selves do it. Two teenagers started throwing cups of soft drinks, tossing candies. Someone yelled at them and they quit. It all seemed so loud, as if I was sitting in the stands with them. The air was full of smells, the food and sodas, and the stink of animals. The tent had probably been bought for the carnival from a circus. The aroma of elephants and lions and monkeys and human sweat had soaked into it, tucked in deep when the tent was folded, released now that it was unwrapped. It wasn't a smell that was ever going to totally slip away. The tent and everything under it smelled funky and amazing all at the same time.

Actually, I was a little ripe myself, having, along with the rest of our team, made a few laps around the rink just to get a feel. It wobbled some. I wobbled some myself. I felt weak-kneed.

I could see Mama and Grandma and Frank and Herb in a front row. They waved at me. I looked for High Top and Dad, but didn't see either one.

I watched as everyone on our team finished their laps and we all gathered in the center with Elbert, who had a towel clutched in both fists, twisting it into a tight coil of cloth.

We hadn't seen the opposing team yet, but Bob had gone back to see if he could get a glimpse before they came into the tent. It probably didn't matter, but Bob wanted to know what we were up against.

"Sit down," Elbert said.

The five of us girls sat on the bench, our two ringers sat in the chairs. Elbert looked us over.

"All right, girls," he said. "Fender Lizards. This is the big one. I thought it might be a good idea to give you names."

"Names?" Gay said. She was sporting a black eye from last night when she caught the elbow, and frankly, I was surprised she was still with us.

Elbert nodded. "Yeah. We got Thunder Bomb and Lightning Strike here, and when the other team comes out, they'll read their names off, and they'll all have nicknames. I thought if we said Gay and Dot and Raylynn and Sue, it lacked a certain something. So I've written down the names I'm going to turn in. Dot, you're Jet. That's because you skate fast. Gay, Helen of Destroy."

"That sucks," Gay said.

"You're Helen of Destroy," Elbert said, "and that's that. Raylynn, Dyno-mite."

"She got a good name," Gay said.

"Hush, Gay," Elbert said. "Miranda you're Little Gorgo."

"What's a Gorgo?" Miranda said.

"It was a monster in Japanese movie," he said.

"Sweet," Miranda said.

"Sue, you're Baby Hammer."

"I'm not sure what that means," Sue said. "But alright."

"Know your name if it comes over the speaker," Elbert said. "Might be nice to know who they're talking about. There will be a guy on the speaker keeping people up with the action."

"Can't they see what's happening?" Sue said.

"It's just a thing to keep the crowd worked up," Elbert said. "Now, you all know your positions. Any questions?"

We looked at one another.

Nothing.

"All right," Elbert said, looking at the ringers. "You two have anything to say?"

"Don't get killed," Thunder Bomb said.

"Okay," Elbert said. "Good advice."

About that time we saw Bob open the gate on the far side of the rink, come through, close it back, and hustle over to us. When he got to us, he said, "I saw them."

"And?" Elbert said.

"Well, the rumor was they were a bunch of juvenile delinquents, or at least looked like it, but after seeing them, I can say that they look more like prisoners the governor commuted off of death row. I thought I saw their tattoos crawling."

"Damn, Bob," Elbert said. "That doesn't boost moral."

"Actually," Bob said, "I sort of felt I was playing it down."

Elbert looked at us. "They're not that bad. They're just girls, like you."

"Only older and meaner and bigger," Bob said.

"It's in the team work," Elbert said. "And we haven't seen them skate, so we don't know how mean they are. How good they are."

About that time the guy with the white cowboy hat came walking up to the gate across the way. He had on a yellow cowboy suit tonight, and his boots were yellow leather, shiny as the sun. He opened the gate, and then we heard the whirl of wheels, and along the side, outside the rink, on the wooden path in front of the bleachers, we saw the other team, THE CARNY KILLERS, they were called.

When they came through that open gate and skated out on the rink, the crowd went wicked crazy, standing and cheering and throwing popcorn and the like. The Carny Killers beat on their chests and let out a yell so loud and scary I have to admit, my bowels went loose.

(45)

*T*he *CARNY KILLERS were* mostly bigger than us, except one, a black girl who was low to the ground and wide at the shoulders, looked like she could pull you out of your skin, toss your bones away.

They started around the track, showing out, getting cheers. They went faster and faster. The wheels on their skates sang. It was a perfect sound, everyone working together. As they made their second round, they all turned their heads toward us and smiled and pointed, said together: "You."

The one in the lead, Death on Wheels, had a mouth piece that had teeth painted on it; big nasty teeth. She had her hair pulled back and tied up with a piece of leather.

"We're dead," Gay said.

"They're just trying to scare you," Elbert said.

"It's working," Gay said.

"Look, they look tough, and they can skate pretty," Elbert, "but what else they got?"

"Team work," Sue said.

"Experience," Miranda said.

"Well, we got heart," Elbert said.

"Mine's in my mouth," Raylynn said.

"Just play the way we practiced," Elbert said.

"Mostly with Cub Scouts," I said.

"You girls got it in you," Lightning Strike said. "Maybe tonight, you want it bad enough, we can pull you out of the fire, if you listen and watch us, and you reach way down deep inside for the glory."

The announcer started up then, calling out the names of the other teams skaters: DEATH ON WHEELS, BLOODY MARY, ROCKET SHOT SAM (Samantha to her friends, he said), LADY DRACULA, ROLLING DOOM, TINA TORNADO and last but not least, BETTY DIES. Betty was the short, stout black girl. She was their jammer.

They skated off, not down into the center with us, but one behind the other until they went right back out of the gate the cowboy was holding open. They piled up there, waiting. The cowboy looked at Elbert and smiled. Elbert shot him the finger.

"That's not very nice," I said.

"Yeah," Elbert said, "but it felt good."

Bob said, "I let you girls off work a lot, so try not to get killed, because come tomorrow, I'm going to need some of you back there, carrying trays."

"Thanks for the pep talk," I said.

"Okay," Elbert said. "You girls warmed up some, but now it's time for you to go out there and skate. Here's the line up."

He told us how to go, and I was last in line, since I was the jammer. That's how Elbert wanted to play it. He gave Bob the list with our new names on it. Bob took it over to the announcer, and we went out on the rink in the planned order.

We went around once, and when we went around the second time, we were low down and skating hard, and as we passed the Carny Killers, without any of us having planned it, we all turned our heads and looked at them and grinned, and I started up with a yell, and then the other girls followed. We skated faster and faster around the rink, and when we passed them again, we all let out with a war hoop that shook the tent; it was maybe louder than the one the Carny Killers had given out. Gay kicked up one leg and grabbed her ankle as she did, going around on one skate. She kept her leg held up, tossed back her head, styling.

When we skated back to the center, Elbert said, "That's the way to go, girls. You plan that little stunt, Gay?"

"Ballet lessons," she said. "It just came to me."

The announcer went on with some talk about this and that, about how Marvel Creek was a great town, him saying that without having to live there, and then he asked the crowd were they ready for some serious roller derby action.

The crowd let out with cheers and hoots and yells and foot stomping on the bleachers. They sounded a lot more ready than we were.

Elbert looked at Lightning Strike and Thunder Bomb. He said, "I'm going to start with you two, Gay, Raylynn and Dot. Sue, you and Miranda will hold out until later."

"Well," Sue said, "you get me in as soon as you can. I figure I'll get rid of my butterflies soon as I'm out there and get hit. Or lose an eye."

"I feel very similar," Miranda said, "without the eye loss part."

"On the track," Elbert said.

(46)

On the track we got into our positions, me and their jammer at the back, ready to rock and roll. I glanced out at the crowd, searching. And then I saw him. Dad. Top row on the far side. I tried to look at him without him seeing me look, like it was a casual glance. But he saw me. He had his hands on his knees and he lifted one of them in a small wave. I acted like I didn't see it.

Someone blew a whistle, and we were off. I felt as if I were skating through a dream made of molasses and cotton. I couldn't hear anything. Everything I was looking at was in a tunnel, the sides closing in on me, dark as the grave. And then the Carny Killer skating next to me, the other jammer, Betty Dies, opened the world to sight and sound again when she said, "What do you like to do after school, little girl, play with dolls?"

Then she was gone like a shot. She was moving past Raylynn before Raylynn knew she was there, getting a point for passing, and there I was, hanging behind like the tail on a kite.

She passed Miranda and then Sue like they were nailed to the floor. I tried to catch up, but the Carny Killers were skating in front of me every time, blocking my path.

Then I saw it. A gap between Death on Wheels and Lady Dracula. It was wide open. Wide, wide open. It was beautiful. It couldn't have been any better had it come with an invitation and a party favor.

I skated fast, my head down low. I felt giddy. As I was about to shoot through that gap I realized I had worried too much. This wasn't that hard.

Just as I was closing fast, about to dart through, those two came together with a snap of their hips. I hit Lady Dracula in the butt with my head because I was down so low. It was like hitting a brick wall. Next thing I knew I was spinning and flying, and then scraping along the track. I went around and around on my rear end, felt like a mouse in a centrifuge.

By the time I got up, Betty Dies had already passed everyone but Gay, who had somehow ended up at the forefront, skating like a demon, probably trying to get away from the whole thing.

I got on my feet and started out again, angry I had been tricked. I glanced up just in time to see Betty skating wide left, Gay on the right.

Just for meanness, Betty Dies looked over at Gay, and she was so loud when she said it, I could hear her clear as a bell. "Don't you got to stop and get that diaper changed, sweetie pie?"

Gay wheeled to the left real hard and came across the track, screaming like a banshee. Betty Dies jerked her head in Gay's direction. That sound Gay was making was enough to lift the hair off your head.

Gay swung her arm out like a log on a chain. It caught Betty Dies just above the nose, on the forehead. It was some lick. It knocked the mouthpiece out of her mouth and into the bleachers, picked Betty up so high her skates swung up and maybe touched the moon. She landed on her butt, rolled along the track like a bowling ball, right into the empty middle.

I thought she was dead for a moment, her nickname more fitting than she could imagine.

Gay was still skating, just going along like nothing had happened. She had a smile on her face. The kind of smile someone who has just slipped a cog might have.

A whistle blew.

Gay was pulled off the track for a foul.

We all ended up in the middle again. The cowboy came over and yelled at Elbert. Elbert yelled back. The guy with the whistle, who I just now realized was a kind of referee, which lets you know how well I knew the game, came over. The announcer was going on and on about this and that. Betty Dies was up and in a chair. Her head was hung. She shook it a little. Her team was around her.

"That's cheating," the cowboy said to Elbert.

"Yeah," Elbert said. "It is. And of course none of your girls would do such a thing."

"Did they?" the cowboy said. "Did they?"

"Give them time," Elbert said.

The cowboy went away.

The referee pointed at Gay, said, "This gal is out, least for a round. We won't take her out altogether if Betty comes back. We got loose rules here."

"No joke," Elbert said.

"She kills someone though," the ref said, "just watch how quick she comes out."

Gay was standing up, looking across at the other team. "I don't like them," she said. Her voice seemed as if it might be coming from some place distant, where it was dark and scary and everyone wore Halloween costumes all the time. She looked like she could take an axe to all of us at any moment.

Thunder Bomb patted Gay on the shoulder, said, "Find your happy place."

Lightning Strike looked over at Betty Dies. "She don't even know what dimension she's in. She's still moving between worlds."

"I really don't like them," Gay said, staring at the other team. "All of them. They are nasty bad people."

"Okay," I said. "Okay, that's all right. It's okay not to like them. Why don't you stay put for awhile, and think about, oh, I don't know, what Thunder Bomb said. A happy place. Something pleasant. Puppies, maybe."

Gay sat down in one of the chairs and kept staring across at the other team. They, to put it mildly, looked mad. If Gay was thinking about puppies, they all wore spiked dog collars.

I turned to Raylynn, mouthed, Oh My God.

"We have created a monster," Raylynn said.

When the ref was gone, Elbert gathered us around him, except Gay, who was still sitting in the chair. Elbert was looking out at the crowd.

"Dot," he said, "you know that lady I told you that threw the green beans at us, back when I was in the derby?"

"Yeah," I said.

"I think I saw her in the stands," he said. "But she'd be really old now. A hundred maybe. Her arm would be bad, don't you think?"

"Elbert," I said. "You're being paranoid. She's not out there. I don't even know her, and I can tell you that."

"Maybe so," he said. "Maybe so. Okay, here's the thing. Go back out there and... Well, skate fast, don't get killed."

"That's some real strategy you got there," I said.

"Look," Thunder Bomb said. "I got a suggestion. That all right, coach?"

Elbert nodded.

"What we do is we all get in the center of the track. We start a snake movement, left to right, weaving, crossing as right and left, wide as we can without getting too far apart. The head of the snake, that will be me, staying steady. The other three swinging left and right in a big wave, the jammer on the tail end, coming up on us fast after the take off. You got to block, though. That's the purpose of the snake. A unit. To make it work better, everyone behind me grab the other girls hips. Jammer on the end, so that Jet has got some serious momentum when we pop her loose."

"They're going to be really mad, aren't they?" Sue said, looking at the other team mounting the track.

"Yep," I said.

(47)

*B*ack on the track, we lined up. Sue was in, Miranda was still out, and Gay was cooling her heels for being mean as a snake.

Beside me was their new jammer, Lady Dracula. She was tall and made of lean muscle. Her hair was died black and her lipstick was black too. Her eyes were painted up so heavy with eye liner I was surprised she could hold her head up.

Betty Dies was still sitting in a chair in the center with her head down. Gay sat across from her. She had turned her chair so she could stare straight at her.

"So," I said to Lady Dracula, "Betty Dies taking a little break?"

"I'll get you," Lady Dracula said. "We'll get you all."

"Who does your tattoos," I said. "A third grader?"

"Oh, that's really rich," she said.

"What I had on short notice," I said.

"Jet," she said, "I'm gonna stall your engines."

The whistle blew.

Around we went again, and Lady Dracula broke out ahead of me. When I tried to pass, she weaved in front. Without looking back, she always seemed to know where I was going. She took another weave and passed Sue, a.k.a., Baby Hammer.

Up ahead, Thunder Bomb was leading our girls, trying to bring them together into that snake-shape plan, but it wasn't happening. Lady Dracula was dodging between our girls, scooting up front, easy as if she was threading a needle.

I saw Raylynn gaze over her shoulder, pick up Lady Dracula's position. Then Raylynn turned, started skating backwards, always in front of Lady Dracula facing her, showing her the war face, passing a few words to her you wouldn't want on your gravestone. Lady Dracula was so preoccupied with Raylynn, so busy trying to express all of her vocabulary, I passed Lady Dracula so quick and so close, another layer of skin cells and we'd have been using the same legs.

Thunder Bomb snapped a look back, gave us the link up nod. Our team started doing just that, all but Raylynn who was still skating backwards, darting in front of Lady Dracula when she tried to pass; that skating backwards trick Elbert had taught us was coming in handy.

Lightning Strike was in front of me. I grabbed her hips. She grabbed Baby Hammer's, and Baby Hammer grabbed Thunder Bomb's hips. We started weaving that snake. We bumped hips against the other team, moved them, but kept clutching to one another. It held.

We rounded the curve, the snake snapped like Thunder Bomb planned, and I broke loose, went around that track so fast I was surprised I didn't see a checkered flag. I lapped all of their team. The crowd cheered.

It was magnificent.

So magnificent we got cocky.

When I came back around again, Lightning Strike said, "Whip."

I knew what that was from watching her and Thunder Bomb do it in practice. It's where a partner you're passing grabs your hand and flings you forward, causing you to gain more speed than you might get in a curve by yourself.

I stuck out my hand and Lightning Strike grabbed it, and as the track curved, she swung me around it. I could feel the wind blowing so hard I thought it was going to take the hair off my head. I straightened out that curve, and kept going straight, which is not what I had in mind. Right before I went over the railing and into the crowd I thought from here on out Grandma was going to have that room in the trailer all to herself.

I don't really remember hitting the railing or going over it, I just remember waking up in the front row stands with a crowd around me.

One of the crowd was my Dad, another was High Top in her shorts and tee-shirt and work boots. The rest of the bunch were my family, and Herb, though there was a little girl with pig tails I had never seen there too.

I looked at High Top. "You made it."

"Yeah," she said.

Dad said, "Dot, are you okay?"

"Define okay." I said.

"Can you sit up?" High Top said.

I sat up.

"Wow," I said. "I saw birds for a minute there. Big ones."

Herb helped me to my feet.

"No broken bones," he said. "You still look great."

"It's the sweat that makes me shiny," I said.

High Top smiled at me, said, "Maybe you're just not playing aggressively enough."

I laughed. That made my stomach hurt where I had hit the railing. The little girl with the pig tails said, "That was funny."

"Thanks, honey," I said. "Appreciate that."

"Are you all right?" Dad said again.

I looked at him. His eyes were wide and his face was wadded up with fear.

"I'm all right," I said, reached out and touched his arm.

"You got to quit this," he said.

"Nope," I said, and turned to the crowd and raised my hands to show I was all right. The crowd cheered.

I climbed down to the wooden floor next to the contact bar, skated to the gate, and went back out on the track, hands held high, the crowd still cheering.

It was a great moment, and everyone of our team got to play. Gay even got brought back in for a while, but from the moment I went into those bleachers, it was down hill.

The Carny Killers beat us like a rented mule after that. The score was forty to twenty. The only good thing I can say about the rest of the night was that nobody died, and we left the track with all our fingers, eyes, and knee caps in the right place.

(48)

In the locker room we sat on benches, taking off our skates. Elbert was there too, standing in the middle. Elbert said, "Well, we lost, and really bad, a little embarrassing at times, but you gave it all you had. And, you got your own locker room."

"I hit someone," Gay said.

"Yes," Elbert said. "You did."

Gay still seemed a little goofy to me. I didn't like the way she smiled.

"We didn't win any money," Elbert continued, "but you can go home tonight and know you played proud."

Raylynn stood up and moved to the center of the room. She held her hand out in front of her. "Broke, but proud," she said. "Fender Lizards, assemble."

We all got up and went to the middle of the room, laid our hand on hers. Elbert came forward and put his on top. He said, "One for one, and one for all."

We yelled it out and let out a roar.

As we finished, the other team came into the locker room. Betty Dies had a knot above her nose about the size of an apple. She walked over to Gay.

Gay glared at her, said, "You come for a fresh one?"

Betty laughed. "No. We came to say you girls are the worse team we ever played. You don't know crap from wild honey, and you skate like a twelve year old birthday party, but you got more heart and soul than a church choir, the lot of you."

"Is that good?" Gay asked, looking back at me.

"It is," I said.

"We'd love another shot to trounce you anytime," said Rocket Shot Sam. She had a face like a wanted poster and she wore a black and gold grill over her teeth. The tattoo of a snake on her bicep seemed to be looking at me.

Betty Dies stuck out her hand to shake.

Raylynn, who was standing close, stuck out hers.

Betty Dies moved her hand, said looking at Gay, "Her first."

Gay slowly lifted her hand and they shook.

The Carny Killers all shook hands then, gave us a nod and grunt and left us alone.

Elbert left and we all got dressed. I walked out with Raylynn and stood under the starry night. Mama and Frank and Grandma had congratulated us and gone on home.

For the team, there was a party at the Dairy Bob. Herb was going to meet me there. Raylynn was going home now. She had left her kids with a baby sitter and had to leave right away. She had somehow managed to buy a different old car. It looked pretty good, though the front bumper was fastened on with duct tape. She said, "I wouldn't have missed this for the world. Thanks, Dot."

"Thanks? We lost."

"One for one, and one for all," she said. "It was pretty nifty. Tomorrow we go back to work and things are like they were, but tonight, they weren't like that. They were different. We got that much going for us. We had a moment we'll never forget."

"We did," I said, and hugged her. "Kiss the kids."

"I will," she said.

I watched her drive away. When the car was gone Dad came out of the shadows of the carnival tent, walking toward me, his hands tucked down in his pants pockets, his head dipped.

"You just missed Raylynn," I said.

"Yeah," he said. "I know. I owe her an apology too, but I thought I'd tell you I was sorry again. I don't have any good answers for you, other than to say I was a coward. I was a coward in that I didn't stick it out. I was a coward in that I didn't tell your mother I couldn't do it anymore."

"I'm going to agree with all that," I said.

He nodded. "Watching you tonight, I know one thing, at least you're not a coward. Gladly, you didn't get that from me."

"If it makes you feel any better," I said, "skating in a roller derby and taking care of a family are pretty different. I know that."

"Still," he said. "I'm proud of you. But I can't come back."

"Mama wouldn't have you back," I said. "Not now."

"Fair enough, but even if she would, I can't come back. I've started over. I've moved on down the road. I shouldn't have, at least not the way I did it, but I have. Things have changed, and there's no going back. It's like getting older. You do it if you mean to or not, and you don't get young again. I'm sorry I haven't been there for you, for all of you."

"All right," I said. I actually wanted to say something else snappy, but to be honest, I'd lost all my steam by then. It was all I could do not to cry.

"I was thinking," he said, "I can't make up for the time I lost, way I handled things, but maybe we could, how do they say it… Have a relationship."

"I don't know," I said.

"I hear you," he said, "and I don't blame you. Not even a little. All I ask is you give me a chance. We can go to lunch or dinner some time. Talk a little. I might find someway to explain things better."

"You can explain things forever," I said, "and they won't be better. I know that now."

"But, we could talk. It could mean something for us to talk."

I nodded. "It might be something we could try."

"A hug?"

"I don't think so," I said. I stuck out my hand.

Dad looked at it hanging out there in the air. He pulled his out of his pants pocket and took mine.

"Okay," he said.

(50)

At the party we ate hamburgers and bragged on the good stuff we had done. Gay thought maybe she didn't want to be a model anymore, that maybe she wanted to be a derby queen.

We told her to sleep on it.

There was an old time juke box in the Dairy Bob, and Bob turned some records on, that old fifties and sixties stuff he loved, and to be truthful, me too. There was something special about it, like it came from straight from the heart. We danced. Me and Herb together, and sometimes all of us girls dancing at once, including Thunder Bomb and Lightning Strike, who after that night I never saw again.

I had invited High Top, and she showed up, and we talked about studying for the GED, and doing it right away. She danced with Bob, and later that night I saw them sitting on the counter, their feet hanging over the side, their heads close, smiling. I wasn't sure if I was happy or yucked by that turn of events.

By the end of the night, my ankle where I had twisted it was swollen a little.

Herb followed me home. I half-expected to see Elbert's van there, but it wasn't. When I parked, Herb parked beside me. We got out and stood between the two cars.

Herb said, "You are a wonderfully different kind of girl, Dot."

"I know," I said.

He grinned. "I bet you do."

"You know what?" I said.

"What?"

"How about a kiss?" I said.

"No argument here."

And we did kiss.

To be truthful, we kissed several times.

As Herb climbed back in his car, he said, "See you tomorrow."

"I'm sleeping in," I said, "and then I think I'm just going to hang with the family. But I got your number and no phone, so when I can borrow the one at the Dairy Bob, I'll call."

"I'd like that," he said.

He drove away. I stood there leaning against my car. I looked up at those stars and the moon. It took me a moment to adjust my eyes from the lights in the trailer park, but pretty soon I could see them. They looked clean and white and beautiful. The moon was a sweet, white eye.

I got my skates out of the back of the car and went quietly inside the trailer.

In the dark, I took off my derby clothes and put on my pajamas. As I was climbing into my bed, Grandma rolled over on hers, said, "That's a dumb sport. You know it."

"Yep," I said.

"But," she said, "for a dumb sport, you're pretty good at it."

"Thanks, Grandma."

W/*hen I woke up* it was still dark, but there were pieces of light mixed with the dark, like someone pouring sunshine into chocolate.

I got up and got on my derby outfit, even though it smelled of sweat. I carried my socks and skates with me. I was quiet so as not to wake anyone. I went outside and sat on the steps and put on my socks and laced on my skates and looked at Elbert's van, which had ended up parked there during the night. I was glad to see it.

Light was easing through more solidly now, becoming more vanilla than bloody. I could hear birds singing, and out on the highway just beyond the trailer park, I could hear cars and trucks motoring along.

I climbed off the steps and trudged out past my car on the states, picking my feet up high so I could walk in them. When I got to the concrete drive, I glanced down the length of it. It looked so much shorter than it usually looked.

I started skating. I felt a little stiff, and there was a mild jolt in my ankle, but within seconds it all went away and I felt fine.

I skated down the drive. I thought about how my life had changed. I thought about Dad, and though things weren't perfect with him, I felt a little different about him; at least I was connected, if only by a thread.

I thought about the GED which I planned to ace with High Top's help. I thought about Bob and the Dairy Bob, which I planned to leave for work at High Top's dog charity. But I still liked Bob and I thought he made good hamburgers and not so good fries; that part hadn't changed.

I thought about Elbert, and how he was like a real uncle. A father for that matter. I thought about him and Mama and hoped for the best. I thought about Herb. Thinking about him made me think about a lot of things.

I picked up the pace. The dawn was golden. I ducked my head and skated hard.

I felt swift and powerful.